Riding Shotgun

A little over a hundred yards from the masked desperadoes, Longarm spotted their obvious confusion. He leaned back and chuckled just as the gunman mounted on a pinto fired the first shot. The heavy pistol slug nicked the corner of the iron luggage case, and pinged off into the desert emptiness that closed in behind the coach as it barreled toward danger-filled confrontation.

"Lucky son of a bitch," Longarm yelped, then shouldered his weapon and levered three quick, booming rounds through the Winchester. A deadly accurate series of blasts bounced sharp echoes off Turkey Rock.

The pinto stumbled, then went down in a heap as the coach thundered past the squealing, kicking animal. The animal's rider lay on his side, one leg trapped beneath his wounded mount. He pushed at the saddle with his free food, but appeared unable to break free.

"Mite lucky myself, I guess," Longarm yelled.

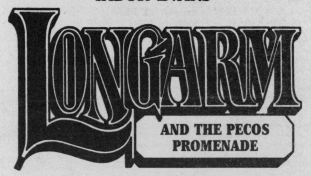

TABOR EVANS

LONGARM

AND THE PECOS PROMENADE

JOVE BOOKS, NEW YORK

THE BERKLEY PUBLISHING GROUP
Published by the Penguin Group
Penguin Group (USA) Inc.
375 Hudson Street, New York, New York 10014, USA

Penguin Group (Canada), 90 Eglinton Avenue East, Suite 700, Toronto, Ontario M4P 2Y3, Canada
(a division of Pearson Penguin Canada Inc.)
Penguin Books Ltd., 80 Strand, London WC2R 0RL, England
Penguin Group Ireland, 25 St. Stephen's Green, Dublin 2, Ireland (a division of Penguin Books Ltd.)
Penguin Group (Australia), 250 Camberwell Road, Camberwell, Victoria 3124, Australia
(a division of Pearson Australia Group Pty. Ltd.)
Penguin Books India Pvt. Ltd., 11 Community Centre, Panchsheel Park, New Delhi—110 017, India
Penguin Group (NZ), 67 Apollo Drive, Rosedale, North Shore 0632, New Zealand
(a division of Pearson New Zealand Ltd.)
Penguin Books (South Africa) (Pty.) Ltd., 24 Sturdee Avenue, Rosebank, Johannesburg 2196,
South Africa

Penguin Books Ltd., Registered Offices: 80 Strand, London WC2R 0RL, England

This is a work of fiction. Names, characters, places, and incidents either are the product of the author's imagination or are used fictitiously, and any resemblance to actual persons, living or dead, business establishments, events, or locales is entirely coincidental.

LONGARM AND THE PECOS PROMENADE

A Jove Book / published by arrangement with the author

PRINTING HISTORY
Jove edition / November 2008

Copyright © 2008 by Penguin Group (USA) Inc.
Cover illustration by Miro Sinovcic.

ISBN: 978-0-515-14546-5

JOVE®
Jove Books are published by The Berkley Publishing Group,
a division of Penguin Group (USA) Inc.,
375 Hudson Street, New York, New York 10014.
JOVE® is a registered trademark of Penguin Group (USA) Inc.
The "J" design is a trademark belonging to Penguin Group (USA) Inc.

PRINTED IN THE UNITED STATES OF AMERICA

10 9 8 7 6 5 4 3 2 1

Chapter 1

Sleep-deprived and suffering from a rye-induced hangover that bordered on Old Testament proportions, Deputy U.S. Marshal Custis Long rolled his stringy, muscled six-four bulk onto one side. A trembling hand snatched at the tattered blanket covering legs decorated with patches of gooseflesh beneath his skintight, cotton long underwear.

He groaned and pulled the moth-eaten coverlet up to his chin. The shivering lawman scrunched himself into a tight, balled-up knot atop the lumpy mattress on his ancient, iron-framed bed. If a single square inch of his body that didn't ache existed, he would have sworn he couldn't feel it. A bone-deep longing for the balmy climes of West-by-God-Virginia darted across his benumbed brain.

Sometime around three a.m. that morning, a fast-moving blast of frigid, ice-tinged, early spring air had swept down on Denver's unsuspecting populace. The storm blustered in from the Front Range of the Rocky Mountains, fifteen miles to the west, and made a man feel like he was being whipped with an icicle the size of an ax handle.

Overnight, Longarm's ramshackle digs on the less-than-fashionable side of Cherry Creek had turned into something akin to a Chicago stockyards meat locker in January. Now, muted, wintry gray light from a creeping sun's dull rays seeped through his rented room's threadbare curtains, but left no comforting heat behind.

One blood-veined eye popped open—then, much slower, the other. He cast a woeful, squinty glance at the tiny, iron, potbellied heater in the corner. The device was cold enough to freeze the stink out of a steaming cow flop. A neat stack of kindling and a fresh scuttle of coal taunted him from a spot beside the idle stove.

Damnation, it's colder in here than a frozen outhouse seat in Montana, he thought. He cursed himself for not building a roaring fire the preceding night, before he'd dropped into bed like a felled aspen sapling watered for a solid year with hundred-fifty-proof Maryland rye.

A tongue that felt about as big as the baggage boot on a Concord coach flicked across the backs of gummy, foul-tasting teeth. A piece of something meatlike and rancid-tasting found its way from between his teeth and onto the swollen appendage. He spit the offending morsel across the room. It hit the front of his dresser and stuck.

"Bah. That's downright turrable. Jus' turrable," he groggily muttered aloud to the empty room. "Looks god-awful, too."

A naked arm snaked from beneath the protection of the blanket, then slithered its way into the frosty air. Trembling fingers pawed the Ingersoll watch off the wobbly bedside table. He drew the big ticker as close to his face as he could. An uncontrollable groan rumbled all the way up from frigid, benumbed toes upon realization that his scheduled appointment with Marshal Billy Vail loomed but a mere hour away.

The heavy timepiece clattered into a metallic heap when he pitched the watch back to its nightly resting spot atop the twin-barreled .44-caliber derringer attached to the opposite end of its glittering gold chain. With a loud sigh of determined resignation, Long flopped onto his back, doggedly pitched the almost toasty cover onto the floor, then hopped out of the bed barefoot.

He yawned, stretched, and growled like a hungry grizzly awakening from a long winter's hibernation. He scratched everything he could find to scratch, then, still stiff and sore-muscled, shuffled across the hardwood floor to the stove. The ragged blanket offered a bit of protection from the frosty, stained, and pockmarked oak boards beneath feet that felt like blocks of ice—not much protection, but a little.

An uncooperative spine snapped into place like kinks in a rusted logging chain as he bent over and opened the dormant heater's squeaky grate. Shredded pieces of old newspaper and kindling got gingerly stuffed inside, then lit with a sulfur match scratched to life on the potbelly's rusted side.

Once the kindling had flared to a satisfactory height, he dropped a handful of coal on the surging flames. Still in a state of half-awake grogginess, he nodded approval of a fine fire-making effort, slammed the grille shut, then turned his backside to the heat for a more even spread to the growing warmth.

He sniffed, then snuffled along one arm like a redbone hound in search of a hidden trail. The barely detectable scent of lilac, still clinging to some parts of his body, set him to mentally blaming Delinda Samson for his current state of hungover, bleary-eyed, soreheadedness. But after less than five seconds of mentally rehashing their extended two-day tussle, he could not help but smile.

They had crashed into one another on the boardwalk outside Denver's Harper House Hotel at Broadway and Colfax. He'd rounded the corner of the building shortly after a refreshing visit to a nearby tonsorial parlor, and damn near run the stunningly beautiful lady over like an uncontrolled, runaway, driverless beer wagon.

The staggered woman squealed in surprise, went over bassackwards, and landed on the dirt- and grime-covered public walkway with a resounding thump. Her clumsy fall exposed an amazing expanse of shapely stocking-and-garter-covered leg. A lack of pantalets gifted him with a fine view of an absolutely spectacular, totally unclothed caboose, and a thick patch of silken, midnight-colored tresses highlighted a dewy-lipped snatch.

"Damn, miss." The epithet escaped his lips before he could bridle a wayward tongue. "Here, let me help you up," he said, grabbing her leather-gloved hand and pulling.

It surprised the hell out of Longarm when the hand he'd failed to focus on came all the way up from the grit-covered planks of the boardwalk and delivered a resounding open-palmed smack across his weathered, deeply tanned face. He rubbed a reddened cheek and grinned. Muscular little gal wasn't much bigger than fryin' size, but she packed quite a wallop.

"What in the wide, wide world of male stupidity were you thinking? Or better yet, do you think at all?" she screeched, then brushed the disheveled netting of her tiny, elegant hat away from narrowed, gunmetal blue eyes. Arched eyebrows looked like gun sights on a Sharps Big Fifty. "Stupid, bumbling clod. Look at the mess you've made," she added, and set to brushing dirt from the front of a stylish, dove gray, ankle-length dress that had recently done so little to cover the carnal treasures hidden beneath.

Longarm's somewhat startled but always interested gaze swept the entire voluptuous package in a single ogling glance. She was just about half a head taller than five feet, raven-haired, and stacked like a brick Montgomery Ward's reading room, with a blindingly white ruffled blouse that tickled the fine-looking female's pointed chin, jaws, and flame-colored ear lobes. Upturned breasts fetchingly jutted from a heaving chest. The whole parcel was cinched into a bone-staved corset so tight it appeared a man could have easily encircled her tiny waist with his hands.

She glared up at her grinning tormentor for a second, then, all of a sudden, twisted around and sent dust flying as she whacked at her deliciously heart-shaped rump.

In a studied display of proper gentlemanly upbringing, Longarm snatched his snuff-colored Stetson off, bowed ever so slightly, and attempted to help her clean the gritty trash from the bottom of her seemingly modest but eye-catching outfit.

"My most humble apologies, ma'am," he said as he flicked his hat at a tiny spot on the nearest of her shapely hips.

She slapped at the invasive hand. "What are you doing? Don't you dare touch me, you big lummox."

Inquisitive people nervously scuttled past the sparring couple as his smile widened. He nodded, then said, "You're entirely right, ma'am. I'm an unthinking, chuckleheaded boob and deserve every ounce of your justifiable wrath." He dropped to one knee. "Would it help mend your wounded pride if you could just haul off and kick the hell outta me right here in front of God and all the hoople-heads a-passin' us on the street? Be a once-in-a-lifetime pleasure to hold my supplicant's posture and endure just about anything to get another look at those striking legs of yours."

The girl abandoned the beating she was giving her well-rounded behind and gazed down at him with a growing degree of interest. The fiery color in her neck and ears appeared to abate a mite. She tossed raven-colored tresses and let out a deep-throated, cackling chuckle.

"Well, now," she said, and flashed an expanse of near-perfect teeth, "I might consider beatin' the bejabbers out of you with a singletree for five or ten minutes, if one were readily available. But only if you'd swear on your honor to hold still long enough for me to do some permanent damage."

Longarm placed the Stetson over his heart, flung an arm out like a singer he'd once seen in a minstrel show, and bowed even lower. "Your obedient servant, dear lady. Additionally, I'm more than willing to help you pick out the instrument of my fully justified punishment." He shot a sneaking glance at the bug-eyed, hat-tipping passersby, then gazed up at the girl again from the corner of one eye. Her belligerent demeanor appeared to have subsided even more. It almost seemed as how she'd begun to realize what an uncommon commotion they'd created on one of Denver's busiest, most peaceable streets.

After a second more of head-tilted consideration, she testily motioned for him to rise. "Do get up, sir. You're embarrassing both of us." A quick side-to-side glance confirmed the curious interest of gawking onlookers.

Longarm stood, then carefully snugged the Stetson back onto his head. A finger slid back and forth under his freshly trimmed mustache, then twirled around one end. "You must allow me to remedy my crude imposition on your totally innocent person, miss. As a true gentleman, I simply cannot, nay, will not, accept no for an answer."

A slight smile begrudgingly etched its way across her flawless face. For the first time, the disheveled girl appeared more than just a little interested in his bold manner. Hands clasped behind her back, she thrust her magnificent chest forward in the most brazenly enticing and fetching manner, then said, "And just how would you propose to do that, sir? And be aware, I simply cannot wait to hear your answer."

6

More here than meets the untrained eye, he thought, then flicked a glance at the hotel's entrance. "Well, now, there's a right fine restaurant just inside the Harper House. Allow me, at the very least, to buy you a cup of coffee, or perhaps a pot of fresh-brewed tea, by way of apology for my craven inattention and the horrible inconvenience I've caused by my callous disregard for your, ah, absolutely beautiful person."

Her concentrated gaze crawled down Longarm's broad, muscular chest, took in the narrow athletic waist, then lingered for several speechless seconds on the bulge in his skintight, tweed britches.

She surprised the apologetic lawman when she leaned so close her mouth almost touched his ear, then whispered, "Why, sir, are you making so bold as to try and seduce me after having already laid me low in the public thoroughfare in front of God and everybody?"

A sly smile creaked across Longarm's open, friendly face. The aroma of lilac, tinged with the powerful musk of moist, female sex, danced around inside his flared nostrils. He let his breath play on her ear for a second, then whispered back, "Why, come to think of it, yes, ma'am. Yes, indeed. More to the point at hand, would you be seduced?" He leaned away, smiled, and waited for an answer.

A snaky tongue flicked over full lips from one corner of her mouth to the other, followed by an invitingly wicked smile. "Oh, you are a bad, bad man, sir. But to answer your audacious question directly—perhaps."

Longarm tipped his hat. "It's true," he said, "when it comes to women as beautiful as yourself, ma'am, I've been known to be a bad, impudent, downright insistent feller. But trust me when I tell you, darlin', even at my baddest, I'm probably the best you've ever accidentally bumped into. Should you concur with my humble proposition, I fully intend to prove that fact in the most efficacious manner you could imagine."

She tossed her black curls again and laughed aloud. A deep, comfortable, accepting guffaw was followed by: "This should really be interesting. Do lead the way, *good* sir."

Five minutes after the passion-struck couple stepped arm in arm across the Harper House's threshold—and with the knowing cooperation of an old poker-playing amigo who manned the hotel's desk—Custis Long and the now-panting girl pushed the door to a second-floor suite aside, slammed it shut, and began ripping at one another's clothing.

No words of endearment were spoken. No romantic overtures evidenced themselves. Laces, belts, snaps, drawstrings, and buttons were loosed, popped, or rent asunder by the heated fury of their raging, unbridled lust.

Hats, boots, shoes, stockings, and other clothing flew about the room. Clothing of all sorts drifted to the colorful Persian carpet below their unfeeling feet like snowflakes in a winter storm. Longarm's pistol belt ended up on the floor, unthinkingly deposited next to his boots.

When his pants and balbriggans formed a puddle around bare feet, the girl's eyes widened with fiery pleasure and pure yearning. She grabbed him, then ran both hands up and down the steely saber of love between his stout legs as though she'd found a new toy to play with.

"Gloriosity. What on earth do we have here? Sweet, Merciful Father in heaven," she yelped, and pulled him nearer by latching onto his stiff rod and tugging. She hunched against the thick appendage. "Don't believe I've ever seen anything to match this. 'Cept maybe in the meat cabinet of a butcher shop. Gimme some."

A toothy, crooked grin split Longarm's lips. "Whatever you say, darlin'. Let's get this show a-goin' and put the one-eyed love weasel to some good and proper use."

The giggling girl let out a trilling squeak. She threw her arms around his neck, hopped into the air, and with the skill of a French watchmaker, slid her splendidly juicy, fur-trimmed cooz onto his enormous, waiting, rock-hard shaft of throbbing, blood-engorged flesh.

Longarm grabbed a cheek of her magnificent ass in each hand and tried his best to assist her surprisingly agile move. In an instant, the fist-sized head of his pulsating dong hit rock bottom of the girl's slick, sopping depths. The black-haired beauty was immediately racked by a noisy, gushing orgasm that fluttered around Long's cock like a covey of alarmed doves.

"Oh, God, but you are a stallion," she moaned into his ear. "Fuck me till I have to crawl to the door like a whipped dog when it comes time to leave."

"Your obedient servant, ma'am," he mumbled, then, without breaking their heated coupling, he hobbled toward the bed and dropped her onto it, then pulled her to the edge of the mattress. While he was still standing, his muscular hips advanced and retreated like a drive rod on a stoked Baldwin steam engine.

He threw his head back and laughed when, eyes tightly shut, she twisted her head to one side, then bit herself on the arm and pulled at the taut skin till it bled. *God Almighty, what a woman,* he thought. And their lusty dance had only just begun.

Chapter 2

After nearly an hour of strenuous, ass-thumping exertion, thumb-sized beads of sweat had popped out all over both the eager participants' overheated bodies. Slick, salty, body fluids flowed in tiny, steaming rivulets along the creases and valleys created by their quick, frenzied, and energetic joining. In a matter of a few additional minutes, the couple's expended exertion resulted in a pair of flushed, sheen-covered bodies that continued to rage at one other like wild animals.

Early in the action, Longarm's impetuous bedmate had reached between lava-hot legs, parted the lips of her dripping sex, and pawed at her fiery notch as though she might very well burst into active flame. She'd easily found the raised, thumb-sized center of her unchecked yearning, and rubbed, stroked, and caressed herself with three fingers, as though there might never be another opportunity. With her free hand she'd cupped a perfectly formed breast, pushed it upward, and begun to suck and lick at its dark, hardened tip and puckered areola. All of that, and more, whilst Longarm's belly and hips made loud, squishy, slapping noises against her spurting glory hole and shapely ass.

The girl's blatantly provocative move, of tongue and

mouth applied to excited, stiffened nipple, spurred Longarm to even greater heights of energetic exertion as surely as if she had applied a leather quirt to the backside of a surging, thoroughbred, Kentucky racehorse.

He stepped out of his useless pants, without missing a single juice-squirting stroke. Kicked them to a spot somewhere beneath the complaining bed, and pushed his way on top of the action for more comfortable access to her gooey, cock-scorching gash. With one hand firmly grasping a spindle in the headboard of the bed, he gazed down at the furious action between their legs and then upped the speed of his thrusts to a new and dizzying level.

Redoubled efforts at pleasing her were amply rewarded when she drew shaking knees up as high as she could, then used her elbows to force them back to the point where they brushed her ears. She craned her neck forward and watched, wide-eyed, the vivid, ass-pounding action at the pit of her being. Another in a seemingly endless series of shuddering orgasms racked the moaning girl from the soles of her feet to the tip ends of her coal-colored hair. Pale blue eyes glazed over, appeared to have flipped into the back of her skull, and she dropped back onto the sweat-dampened pillow as though completely spent.

Longarm slowed, ever so slightly, for perhaps no more than a second. In a display of amazing strength and dexterity, the girl, seemingly worn to the nub, suddenly snapped back to life. She wrestled him onto his back, and went to bouncing up and down and thrashing around on his love muscle like a tormented soul freshly released from Hell's fifth circle of the damned. And then, just as suddenly as it had all begun, she let out a shuddering yelp, absorbed his thunderous climax, flopped onto her side, and went to snoring like an exhausted teamster after a weeklong drunk.

Over the next day and a half, the ardent couple ate,

drank, slept, and went at each other like sex-starved occupants of a deserted Pacific island, but rarely spoke to one another. They did the dirty deed on the floor amidst discarded clothing, standing against the wall, in both available chairs, on top of the dressing table, inside the wardrobe, in a tub filled with lukewarm water, and even back in the bed a time or two.

They sucked each other. Longarm yodeled in the valley. They sixty-nined. Went at it from the front, from the side, from the back, and end to end. Then started all over again, and again, and once again. From all Longarm could tell, yodeling in the valley and that end-to-end business appeared to be the addled girl's two favorite things in the entire world of sinfully wicked carnal behavior.

Somewhere along the way, he gave up counting the number of times he squirted a steaming-hot load into her waiting body, and came to the considered opinion that the wild-assed gal was determined to fuck him to death.

Finally, early on the afternoon of the second day, with the heavy scent of musk-tinged sex oozing from every pore, the girl lay with her head on Longarm's drum-tight stomach. One hand lay lovingly nestled between her own legs, while she worked at sucking him back to life for another sheet-singeing session of vigorous humping.

As though struck by lightning, she suddenly rolled onto one side and gazed into his weary face. With his crowbar of a meat rod still in her hand, she grinned and said, "By the way, what's your name, honey?"

An exhausted Longarm coughed, laughed, then snorted, "Just be royally damned. Was wonderin' if you were ever gonna ask. Had begun to feel like I was being shamelessly used and might well get cast aside. End up slinking into the night, rejected, brokenhearted. Nothing more than an anonymous and quickly forgotten trifle in your travels along life's twisting road." He smiled, arched an eyebrow. "Name's Long, darlin'. Custis Long. And yours?"

"Delinda Samson."

"Well, Delinda, I'm right pleased to make your acquaintance."

"Same here. And what is it you do here in Denver, Custis?" Her tongue flicked around the head of his cock, licked up and down the shaft, then twirled around the engorged head again.

Longarm raised his hips to aid her efforts. "U-h-h-h, I'm a deputy U.S. marshal working out of the First District Court of Colorado."

A look of shocked surprise popped onto Delinda Sampson's face. Longarm's slablike dong slapped against his stomach with a resounding plop. She kicked herself away from layers of sheets and jumped out of the bed. An accusatory finger got shaken in her still-shuddering lover's face as she yelped, "You're a lawdog?"

Custis Long sank into the mattress and flipped a sheet over his nakedness. He casually rearranged the stack of pillows under his head, then leaned over on one elbow. "Yep. 'S true, Delinda. Most folks even call me by my nickname, Longarm. You know, like the long arm of the law. You can call me Longarm, too, if'n you'd like."

Delinda Samson's hands went to her head, as though she thought it might explode. The stark-naked female dripped sex as she paced toward the door, then back again. "Sweet Weepin' Jesus. Of all the men in Denver I could've picked. What the hell was I thinking?"

"Picked? Whatta you mean picked? What's the problem, darlin'?"

"Oh, shit. Don't call me darlin'. Not now. Not after what you just told me. If Pinky finds out about this, he'll kick my aching ass all the way back to Fort Worth."

14

Longarm reached onto the bedside table, retrieved a cheroot, and lit up. He shook the sulfur match out, then said, "Pinky? Who'n the hell's Pinky?"

Delinda stopped pacing, glared at Longarm, and hands fisted on her shapely hips, snarled, "Look, I'm a working girl, Custis. Surely a man of your background knows exactly what that means. Good Lord, did you actually think you'd somehow managed to get lucky with a poor, naïve farm girl who'd just dropped off a turnip wagon out front of the hotel? Pinky's my, uh-h, *manager.*"

"Manager, is he? Well, I must admit I had my suspicions when I *accidentally,* mind you, observed as how you weren't wearin' any underpants. But you never bothered to mention anything as crassly unrefined as price. Besides, I never pass on a good thing, especially when it drops right in my lap—or on my face, as it were."

Delinda Samson fell backward onto the bed as though totally exhausted by the exchange, then let out a ragged sigh. "Well, shit. Truth be told, Custis, I've just been havin' way too much fun. Never had anybody do the big wiggle the way you do it. And I mean *n-o-o-body.*"

"How very kind of you to notice, darlin'."

"Oh, God. This whole dance just kinda came over me all of a sudden like. Our meeting *was* purely accidental, but I figured I might as well go ahead and use it to whatever advantage might present itself. Christ. Probably get the beatin' of my life over this mess. You got any idea how much it usually costs for me to do what we've been doing for the past two days?"

An impish leer flashed across his handsome face. "Not a single clue. Can't be all that much."

She frowned and slapped his leg. "Well, don't go counting on such faulty reasoning. My services aren't cheap. Not by a long damned shot. Just look at me. This only goes to gentlemen of quality. Men who appear well heeled, rich, powerful, or influential. That's why I'm here in the first place. Convention of Western cattle growers is supposed to start up today. Every hotel in town should be full of willing men with wads of money in their pockets. Costs a hundred dollars a night for my services. We've already burned one night up and are about to start working on another."

"Hundred dollars. Helluva lot of money. Sorry to tell you this, beautiful, but I don't pay for pussy. Ever."

"Oh, God. That's just such typical male hoo-hah if I ever heard it. Well, then, this dance is damned well over for sure."

With that, Delinda Samson hopped up, threw on her clothes, and was soon parked in front of the only mirror in the room at work on her hair and face. She glanced at Longarm's still-naked reflection and said, "You gonna get out of bed, or what?"

"Not sure. You've presented me with quite a conundrum, darlin'. Been thinkin' on it. Tell you what I'll do. My upbringing simply will not allow me to let you suffer because of anything I've done, or been a party to. As a consequence, I'm willing to make a gift of fifty dollars to help offset any problems that may result from our little *misunderstanding*. A gift, mind you, not payment for services rendered."

Delinda checked her carefully applied, near-invisible makeup one last time, then turned on Longarm like a cornered wildcat. "Guess that'll have to do, won't it? I can match your fifty with a like amount from savings I've squirreled away. Least that should fend off a thrashing."

"Pinky ever whipped you before?" he asked as he climbed out of the bed.

After a long pause, she shook her head. "No. No, he hasn't. I've always been able to come up with the money.

But, as you well know, there's a first time for everything. Guess this time around, Pinky'll just have to deal with a small shortage."

Once the necessary fifty had changed hands, Delinda flounced her shapely ass to the door and jerked it open. She paused long enough to turn, aim her dazzling boobs at Longarm like twin cannons, and snort, "If we should meet on the street anytime soon, Custis, please God, act like you don't know me."

Standing in the middle of the room, still bare-assed naked, Longarm grinned. "You sure that's what you want, darlin'?"

Delinda's gaze settled on his semirigid prong. An unforced grin appeared on her naturally red lips. "No, not really. Jesus, Custis, you're like a raging forest fire, unquenchable." And just like that, she was gone.

Within minutes of her departure, Longarm had gotten himself put back together, then sprinted from the Harper House and headed for the Holy Moses Saloon on Larimer Street. He spent the rest of that day and most of the night at a poker table.

In the process of winning nigh onto two hundred dollars, he drank a tubful of rye whiskey, smoked a dozen of the nickel cheroots he favored, and finally stumbled home in the wee hours of the morning. He'd hoped to fall into the comforting arms of the saloon's owner, Cora Anne Fisher. But bartender Mike O'Hara had reluctantly informed Longarm that the lady was out of town and wouldn't be back for at least a week.

Now, bone-tired from a few nights of way too little sleep and way too much of everything else, he swayed in the frigid, knee-knocking dank of his room. He smelled of soured liquor, cheap tobacco, and the still-faint but compelling musk of Delinda Samson. A quick, basin rinse in ice-cold water and a dash of bay rum did little to help the situation, but it was the best he could do.

Longarm glared at his reflection in the smoky, badly silvered mirror over the dresser while pulling on a fresh, gray flannel shirt in his gradually warming digs. The daily ritual of getting dressed, which he'd followed for his entire adult life, continued when he draped a shoestring tie around his neck. He slipped into a tweed vest, then sat on the edge of the bed and wrestled a pair of brown tweed pants over the skintight long underwear that had kept him from freezing his nuts off the night before. Next came two pairs of socks to ward off the creeping Colorado cold outside. Nothing worse than frigid feet and freezing toes. Then, low-heeled stovepipe cavalry boots.

Nearly completely dressed, Longarm gamely stood again, moved to the other side of his ratty bed, retrieved the supple cordovan leather gun belt from the bedpost above his pillow, and strapped it around his waist. The well-used cross-draw rig settled nicely in a comfortable spot just above narrow hipbones.

A quick check of the loads of the Colt .44 Lightning completed a vital part of his daily regimen of tasks that could easily mean the difference between life and death. He set the cylinder of the weapon spinning and shoved it into its well-oiled cradle. The watch and two-shot derringer, joined together by the gold chain, were recovered from the bedside table and placed in separate vest pockets, which finished out the desired look and feel of comfort and safety.

He rummaged around and found a clean, pressed linen handkerchief in a top drawer of his bureau, and slipped it into the pocket of his frock coat. His Colorado-styled snuff-colored hat was precisely centered on his head and tipped a bit forward in a rakish cavalry officer's fashion.

"Look almost human now," he said to his own image in the mirror.

He shoveled two more scoops of coal into the stove, damped the fire down as low as he could, and hoped the barely smoldering flames would keep the room warm the rest of the day.

On the way out the door, he grabbed his shearling coat from the wardrobe, then slipped into lambskin's comforting warmth as he silently crept down the rooming house's creaky stairs. Aware that some of his neighbors might still be abed, the groggy, fuzzy-brained lawman felt compelled to respect their peace and quiet.

Outside, beneath the barren branches of a struggling, cottonwood, Longarm lit a nickel cheroot and puffed it to life. The blustery air wafting down from the Rockies' frozen peaks snapped him awake with a chilling slap in the face that went right to the soles of his boots.

"Sweet Jesus," he muttered to the whistling wind in a puff of cigar smoke and icy breath. Flecks of wet snow landed on his mustache, stuck, and didn't melt. "Colder'n I thought," he grumped. "Gonna be like Hell with the furnace off tonight."

A pair of soft roper's gloves felt mighty good as he pulled them over rapidly numbing fingers. He stuffed his hands inside the heavy leather coat's pockets and clenched his teeth down on the cheroot, then buried his chin in the shearling's furry collar. With the cheroot protruding at a jaunty angle from tight lips, he heeled it for Colfax Avenue.

The cinder path along Cherry Creek crunched like breaking glass beneath Longarm's feet until he reached Denver's newly laid stretch of red sandstone sidewalk. The handsome walkway led east to Billy Vail's office in the Federal Building on Colfax near Colorado's gold-domed State Capitol.

A grumbling stomach almost drove the single-minded lawman to one of the numerous independent food vendors along the street. But the bracing cold, and a well-earned reputation for tardiness, drove him to hurry along the thoroughfare's crowded walkway like a Denver & Rio Grande freight on a downhill grade.

Chapter 3

Longarm forced himself to run up the Federal Building's front steps, then took the marble, interior stairway to the second floor two steps at a time. He flung the door to Billy Vail's outer office open. His action, punctuated with great force, caused the marshal's surprised clerk, Henry, to drop a heaping shovel of coal on the floor while in the process of stoking the office's huge heater.

"Good Lord in Heaven, Marshal Long, you scared the bejabbers out of me," the bespectacled Henry complained, then slammed the grate shut on the massive Colonial-model iron stove. The fire-belching beast appeared three times the size of the tiny potbelly in Longarm's spartan Cherry Creek room.

Longarm smiled for the first time that morning as he shucked his gloves, shearling coat, and hat, then hung them on a convenient but already overburdened rack just inside the office's main doorway.

Vigorously rubbing his hands together, he turned back to Billy Vail's symbolic right arm and said, "Who'd you think I wuz, Henry? Some kinda crazed, murderous Santy Claus swept into your toasty-warm office on an icy, evil wind from the misty tops of the Rocky Mountains."

"No. Of course not," the temperamental clerk snapped. Then he began fussily sweeping the sooty mess he'd made back onto his coal shovel with a short-handled fireplace brush. "Just a bit nervous this morning, Longarm, that's all—a bit nervous and flusterated."

"Nervous. Flusterated. What've you got to be nervous about? Good God, man, you work in a nice warm office. Got a big, fine, comfortable leather chair to sit in all day. Don't have to worry 'bout nobody shootin' at you, 'less you're seein' some married lady and ain't told me 'bout her yet."

The persnickety clerk sniffed. "Well, I never."

"Aw, hell, Henry, you don't even have to write your letters by hand no more. You can whip 'em out on that newfangled, clickety-clackin' typewritin' machine on your incredibly neat desk. Seems to me as how you're squattin' in some mighty tall cotton, my friend. Gettin' paid to do a job like yours oughta be against the law."

Henry rolled his owl-like eyes in disgust, dumped a shovel of billowing, black dust into the glowing stove's glowing mouth, and slammed it shut. As he fussed with the damper handle on the flue, he said, "Marshal Vail's not feeling well today. Must admit I'm very concerned about the man's health. From all available appearances, he will most certainly have to see a doctor some time soon. Given his delicate condition, I fear he might well have to be admitted to the hospital later this afternoon."

Longarm's concerned glance darted to Billy Vail's partially opened inner office door. "Delicate condition, eh? He in there now, Henry?"

The anxious paper pusher flounced back to his leather throne and flopped into it, as though tired to the bone. "Of course he is, Longarm. Where else? He's been patiently awaiting the arrival of his most consistently tardy deputy to receive an important assignment. Soon as this meeting is over, I'll probably have to rush him to the nearest available physician."

Longarm straightened his jacket and vest, then strode across the room to the door of Billy Vail's private office and pushed his way inside. His pasty-faced, puffy-eyed boss stood at the far end of an overloaded mahogany desk, feet apart, leaning forward with one hand braced on each corner as though he might be about to collapse.

"What the hell's wrong with you, Billy? Henry says you ain't feelin' none too good. Sure as hell don't look all that great. That's for damned sure. 'Course you never have looked all that good to me anyways."

Vail glanced up at Longarm like an abandoned hound dog whose family had moved away and left him to the whims of a cold and heartless world. "Well, you don't look that stellar either, Deputy U.S. Marshal Custis Long. Those dark rings under your eyes and all that chin stubble give you a recently awakened coonish aspect."

Longarm toed at the carpet. "Well, I must confess as how I ain't had all that much in the way sleep in the past three days or so. Keepin' company with wild, hot-assed women, drinkin' too much, gamblin', stayin' up way too late—usual kinda things for me. What's your excuse, Billy?"

A racking shudder appeared to pass through Vail's entire body like a peaking wave on the ocean before he said, "Pretty much the same thing, Custis. Can't sit down. Been standin' up, day and night, for damn near a week. Haven't slept a wink the entire time."

"Cain't sit? Why not?"

Vail grimaced. He brought himself almost upright, but

23

stopped short, as though knives sliced at his backside. Then he carefully turned and waddled to the double window behind his desk like a turtle dragging a broken leg.

With a single finger he pushed the heavy curtain aside, stared at the pedestrians below on Colfax Avenue for a second, then said, "Got a carbuncle the size of a guinea egg in the crack of my lardy ass, Custis. Just about the most painful thing I've ever suffered with in my entire life. Getting worse by the minute. Burns like Hell's eternal fires. Feels like maggoty, flaming worms are crawlin' 'round in my ass."

Custis Long dropped into the tack-decorated Moroccan leather chair that faced Billy Vail's desk. "Aw, come on now. Little ole pimple on the ass cain't be that bad. Be willin' to bet it's nothin' more'n loafin' 'round here all the time that's turned you into a big ole pantywaist. Gotta remember, Billy, the shy dog don't get no biscuits. Need to get your sad self outta this stifflin' dump of an office and ride a thousand miles or so ever once in a while."

"Not today, by God. Gonna have to get someone to look at this throbbing sucker pretty damned quick. Big son of a bitch's killin' me."

"Aw, come on now, Billy."

"Hell, I've been shot more than once, as you well know. Stabbed a time or two. Trampled by horses. Run over by a wagon when I was no bigger'n a nubbin. But you just can't imagine the pain. Trip to the fuckin' toilet's turned into a whole new and dreaded experience."

Longarm screwed his face into a shocked mask, then grinned and said, "Shit, that's way more'n I either needed or wanted to know. Ooops. Didn't mean to make a bad pun there. 'Cause I do feel for you. Can see you're in pain. And you know I love you like a brother, Billy. Even so, I ain't about to be the one to take a look at that big, broad bohunkus of yours. Never have been able to work up much of a desire

24

for starin' at another man's pimple-covered, hairy ass. 'At's why God made doctors."

"Yeah, feel kinda like the tenderfoot who was bein' instructed in how to treat a rattlesnake bite. Ole-timer says, 'All you gotta do is make some cuts across the puncture wounds, then just suck out the poison.' Tenderfoot studied on it for a second and said, 'But what if the snake bites you in a spot you can't get at to suck the poison out?' Ole-timer says, 'Well, that's when you find out who your real friends are.'"

Vail's strained chuckle got cut short by another shuddering wave of pain as he turned from the window and stumble-stepped back to his desk. "Always liked that joke," he said, then gingerly bent over like his spine might break and picked up a thick sheaf of papers. He pitched them into Longarm's lap and quickly grabbed the top of the desk again. Sweat popped out on the paunchy marshal's deeply knitted forehead.

Muscles in Billy Vail's jaws twitched. Through gritted teeth, he said, "All required instructions, necessary letters of introduction, travel documents, and such are in that envelope. All you gotta do is read 'em and light out. Or don't read 'em. Hell, I'm beyond caring right now."

Without opening the pile of papers, Longarm slapped them against his leg. "Hope you're sendin' me somewhere south of Denver, Billy. Truth be told, I'd be happy with just about anywhere south."

Vail's face suddenly turned into a mask of pain. To Longarm, his boss looked like someone who'd just had a hot fireplace poker jammed up his behind. The chief marshal shook from head to foot like a willow tree in a heavy wind, then said, "Well, you're in luck, Custis. Sending you about as far south as you can go and still be in the country. That is, if you call Texas part of the United States. Not quite Hell itself, but damned close."

"Oh, God, Billy. You're not sendin' me to Eagle Pass, Del Rio, Ruidosa, or some equally godforsaken place, are you?"

Vail tried to straighten up, made a move like he wanted to rub his sore backside, appeared to think better of such an action, then fell back to leaning on his desk. "No, it's not quite that awful. Want you to head out to Pecos soon as you can hop a Denver and Rio Grande flyer to Trinidad. Atchison, Topeka and Santa Fe on to El Paso. You know the drill from there."

Longarm's throbbing head lolled around on his neck as though it had somehow come unattached. He sounded like a whipped dog when he moaned, "Southern Pacific to Sierra Blanca. Narrow-gauge to Toya. Ass-bustin' twenty-mile Conklin Brothers coach ride on east to Pecos."

"Yep. That's the ticket, Custis."

"You know, I was just kiddin' when I said you could send me south, Billy."

"Sorry, but I'm not kiddin', not even a little bit."

"You mean to tell me we don't have anything closer to Denver goin' on? Little job up in Boulder? Maybe Fort Collins? Glenwood Springs, yeah, now that's the ticket. I've always liked Glenwood Springs. Know a gal named Betty Caldwell in Glenwood Springs. Suck the paint off a wagon wheel. Bet this pesky cold snap's already passed through there and the sun's shining again. Criminals probably be poppin' up like springtime daisies."

"Doesn't matter if lawbreakers are multiplyin' like rabbits in Glenwood Springs. You're going to Pecos."

"Well, shit. What the hell's goin' on in Pecos, Tejas, that requires the attention of a deputy U.S. marshal of my caliber and fame?"

Billy Vail cast a miserable glance at the banjo clock on

26

his wall, then turned back to his unhappy, soreheaded deputy. "Somebody's been robbing the stage between Pecos and Toya on the west—Pecos and Barstow on the east."

Longarm snorted with disgust. "You're gonna send me all the way to Bum Fuck, Texas, to investigate some backwater pissant stage robberies?"

"Thieves are stealin' U.S. mail pouches, Custis. That particular wrinkle makes the thievery our problem. On top of the numerous thefts, whoever's doin' 'em killed a driver last week. Shot him off the coach, then trampled him to death once he'd hit the ground."

"Damn."

"Bein' as how the mail pouch was the dead feller's responsibility, kinda makes him an unofficial employee of the postal service. Can't have folks goin' around stealin' from the Federal Government and killin' unofficial staff members."

"I can understand the need to stop the thievery, but this *unofficial employee* bullshit's pretty thin, ain't it, Billy?"

"Might be thin, but it'll work just the same. Besides, an official request for assistance came directly from the local constabulary. County sheriff's a feller name of Bud Miller. He and the city marshal, Manny Frazier, both signed the letter. Say they've got their hands full with a rash of stock theft goin' on all over Reeves County. Can't be bothered with trifling irritations like theft of the federal mails and murder."

"Sounds a bit suspicious, don't it? Convenient at the very least. Hell, I've known Manny Frazier for years. Always seemed like a reliable sort. Hell with any kinda weapon."

"Suspicions are for backyard gossips. What we need are facts. That's why you're going to Pecos."

Longarm stood, tapped the sheaf of papers against his thumb, turned, and headed for the door. His fingers had barely touched the knob when Vail said, "I'm probably gonna be out of circulation for a spell, Custis. Get on that business as quick as you can. Don't sit around for a week while I'm down for the count."

Without looking back, Longarm said, "Don't worry, Boss. Be on my way south first thing in the mornin'. Sooner I get to some warm weather, cold *cerveza,* and hot señoritas, the better I'm gonna like it."

He carefully pulled the door to Billy Vail's private office closed, then stomped over to Henry's desk. He shook his finger in the clerk's face and snapped, "Get Billy to a sawbones quick as you can. Man's sufferin' the tortures of the damned and needs something done 'bout it. Wait much longer and the corruption in that boil could get infected."

Henry stopped pecking on his newfangled typewriting machine and used a single finger to push wire-rimmed glasses back up on the bridge of his nose. "Way ahead of you, Marshal Long. We have an appointment with a doctor in less than an hour. Just waiting for him to finish up with your assignment."

Longarm nodded, jammed the sheaf of papers into the pocket of his frock coat, then retrieved his hat and shearling coat from the overloaded rack.

On his way out the door and over his shoulder, he said, "Good. Very good, Henry. Appreciate your dedication. You take care of 'im. I'll check in just as soon as I get back from Hell's asshole—sorry, I meant West Texas."

Chapter 4

After so many years of riding the rails, the rattle and clatter of a near-empty passenger car, moving along the grand ribbon of steel that led just about anywhere, had the power to put Longarm to sleep within a matter of minutes after his butt hit a day coach's uncomfortable, barely padded seat.

He'd grown accustomed to the smell of grease, oil, and burning coal. He immediately relaxed to the hypnotic rocking and the familiar sounds of the train. For Longarm, a trip on the rails usually proved the rough equivalent of being drugged by a heavy dose of laudanum.

Upon boarding, he picked a spot closest to the stove at one end of the car, and piled his canvas possibles bag, saddle, bedroll, rain slicker, and Winchester hunting rifle on the leather-padded bench facing him. Then, the still-tired lawman propped his feet up, settled into the warmth of his shearling coat, and covered tired eyes with his hat. He dozed off less than five miles outside Denver. For the next six hours, he slept like the proverbial newborn babe.

He awoke, somewhat refreshed, when a rake-handle-thin, hatchet-faced conductor with a voice like a foghorn marched down the swaying coach's aisle and announced, "Trinidad, folks. Next stop, Trinidad. Trinidad's the place. If you're gettin' off in Trinidad, load your pistols and hold on to your wallets. Next stop, Trinidad and all points south."

Longarm forced a smile, but thought to himself that he was glad to be one of those disembarking. The one thing he didn't particularly need was a train conductor with a comic twist to his otherwise inconsequential personality. In spite of himself, though, he wondered what the man would find to joke about next.

Perhaps more importantly, he had to admit the mouthy conductor's advice was well founded. Outlaws and thieves of every stripe flourished in Trinidad like buffalo grass on the great American prairie. Pimps, whores, swindlers, and bandits seemed to multiply like rabbits. A prudent man needed to keep a tight grip on anything valuable while walking the town's rough and often life-threateningly dangerous streets.

It took two trips, but the cramped-muscled lawman finally moved his unwieldy pile of belongings off the Denver & Rio Grande rail line's passenger car and onto the Trinidad depot's spacious loading platform.

The outside air had warmed a smidgen, but not all that much. The Atchison, Topeka and Santa Fe train on to El Paso would be along soon—he hoped. The one thing about rail travel that could get Longarm's dander up like a teased rattlesnake—and that he had damned little tolerance for—was any sort of unexpected, unexplained delay. Delays couldn't be avoided, of course, and on an intellectual level he knew it. But sitting on his bony ass wasting time because of someone else's stupidity, neglect, or incompetence just chapped his cheeks. Mechanical failure was another problem altogether, but rated even more ire as far as Longarm was concerned than common, everyday human frailties.

Just outside the depot's official ticket office and window,

the still-groggy lawdog stacked his goods on a wooden bench. So hard a tomcat couldn't scratch it, the slatted seat appeared to have been recently painted a deep, glistening forest green.

He stretched out beside the mound of his personal belongings and lit another square-cut cheroot. He puffed the stogie to life and watched as travelers scuttled back and forth in their concentrated rush to get somewhere else— perhaps anywhere else.

For about an instant, he let his mind drift back to his last stop in Trinidad and the events surrounding a bloody encounter with City Marshal Mason Dobbs and the ghost of Black Mesa, Spook Lomax. But, thank God, that trip to Trinidad was all past, he thought. On to other problems.

The railroad station and bustling loading platform appeared some busier than he remembered from that previous layover. Gamblers, whiskey drummers, stock buyers and sellers, cattlemen, cowboys, loose women of every stripe, and even some reputable-looking ladies, moved back and forth in a constantly churning elbow-to-elbow surge of preoccupied travelers, scam artists, and those who just liked to hang around.

Rumors had it that the town had about hit its peak, and so it amazed him how busy the peckerwood-sized depot still was. But the roiling throng soon thinned out to no more than a handful of wrinkled, bleary-eyed, coach-weary folks who didn't look all that anxious to trade tedious, passing pleasantries with anyone about any topic.

Twenty minutes or so after disembarking, the dozing Longarm's peace and contentment were disturbed by a noisy, loudmouthed row toward one end of the loading platform, near an overburdened baggage cart. A short, nattily dressed gent of about fifty who Longarm took to be a whiskey drummer, or perhaps a salesman of lace-trimmed, ladies undergarments, had a filthy-faced, screeching urchin by the earlobe. Like a Mississippi snapping turtle, the drummer didn't appear inclined to turn him loose until God-sent thunder and blue-tinted lightning had manifested themselves.

Teeth gritted, Longarm twisted in his seat to get a better gander at the action, then smiled when he was able to discern most of what was being said.

"Give it back, you thieving little son of a bitch, and be right goddammed quick about it," the nattily dressed drummer yelped.

"Shit, that hurts. Lemme go, you stupid ole bastard," the scamp cried, then went back to kicking and squealing again.

"Not till you give it back, by God. Twist this ear off, then do the same for the other one, if'n it's not in my hand in ten seconds. Place a right high premium on that bauble."

"Ain't got nothin' of yern, mister," the kid squawked. "Turn me loose, goddammit. Best do 'er quick. I got friends, you know."

The natty gent smacked the brat on the back of his head with an open palm. The sharp rap to the noggin sounded like a pistol shot. "Also got a right filthy mouth on you, boy. 'Pears to me as how you're in serious need of a good mouth-washing with a bar of lye soap. Bet that'd put a halt to most of the filthy language outta you and go miles toward settin' you back on the straight and narrow."

The struggling urchin remained unfazed. "Best let me go, by God. Have my partner kick yer stupid ass all the way from here to downtown El Paso. Gar-un-damn-tee you'll wish you'd never laid a limp-wristed hand on me."

The natty gent threw his head back, laughed, then glanced around the near-empty platform. "Partner? What partner. I don't see any nonexistent partner."

The raucous back-and-forth disagreement had gone on

for some seconds when a burly thug, with a face like the south end of a northbound armadillo, stepped from the noon-day shadows at the far end of the baggage cart. The man looked like you could bounce cannon balls off his head with little effect.

The stubby butt of an enormous cigar jutted from one corner of the ruffian's twisted mouth. In a boldly aggres-sive act, he casually pulled his shabby coattail back to reveal a long-barreled Schofield-model Smith & Wesson pistol jammed behind a thick leather belt.

Around the soggy remains of his stogie, the bent-nosed, scar-faced lout grumbled, "Let the kid go, you dumb-assed little bastard."

Barely half the thug's size, the clearly irate salesman snorted back, "I won't, by God. Thieving little skunk stole my watch. Came right up to me on the pretense of selling sugar tits to hungry travelers looking for a tasty snack. Somehow lifted a solid-gold watch the size of a man's fist from the pocket of my vest."

The kid's bodyguard waved the drummer's remarks aside as though swatting pesky flies away. "Ain't a-listenin' to me, are you, mister? Done said fer you to turn 'im loose. Best do as yer told or suffer some mighty extreme consequences, by God."

"And I've done told you that I won't, you ugly gob of spit. He stole a valuable timepiece from me. Big ticker was awarded to me by my employer in recognition of twenty-five years of good and faithful service. I want it back, by God, and will not capitulate on this issue until I once again have the watch in hand."

The word "capitulate" appeared to confuse the kid's thick-necked, pistol-carrying accomplice. He shook his anvil-shaped head like a longhorn steer with a tick in its ear, then leveled a filthy-nailed finger at the dude. "Done tole you more'n once, mister, turn the kid loose. Yer a-hurtin' 'im. Don't go an' make me bust a cap in your stupid ass."

Longarm cast a pleading glance skyward. He was a serious practitioner of the old philosophy of live and let live, especially when it came to infractions outside Billy Vail's assignments, but his unstinting devotion to duty had reared its many-tentacled head.

"Why me?" he groaned to an empty, cloudless sky, but got no answer. "Where the hell's the local constabulary when you need 'em?" Still no answer. Nothing overhead but the limitless expanse of God's blue heaven.

As though burdened with the weight of a lawless, ungovernable world, the weary marshal stood, flicked his well-chewed but unfinished cheroot aside, then ambled toward the boisterous disagreement. *God, but I hate to get involved in a silly, trivial mess like this,* he thought. In Longarm's opinion, idiotic disagreements had an uncommon and deadly way of turning out badly, no matter how you approached them.

Even a fool could see that the natty gent, while very likely in the right, was overmatched and outgunned—a bad combination in such a difference of opinion, if there ever was one. The situation was, to put it bluntly, the kind of dustup that held the unknowable potential for getting a man killed deader than coyote bait in the blink of an eye.

Using his left hand, Longarm waved and, with a toothy grin, said, "Hold on now, fellers. Let's don't go and do anything foolish. It's way too nice a day to get all worked up and out of sorts over an issue that I'm sure can be solved to everyone's satisfaction in a matter of mere seconds."

Longarm felt he'd been right pleasant by pointing out the obvious, and gave himself an invisible pat on the back. It didn't take long to realize that his overly optimistic assessment was grossly misplaced. What warned him was something he spotted in the thug's eyes: a flat, dead, soulless look that made the hair stand up on his neck. The prickly feeling that death had come for a visit crept up his back and left a path of cold gooseflesh from his waist to his ears.

Chapter 5

The grim-faced thug slanted a surprised, arch-browed glance in Longarm's direction, spit the gooey glob of the cigar butt onto the dusty platform beneath his feet, then said, "Stay the fuck outta this dance, mister. What's goin' on 'tween me'n that asshole yonder ain't no concern of yern. Misunderstanding, if'n they truly 'ere one, is a-'twixt mc'n the dude."

"Yeah, stay the fuck outta our business, you lanky pile of walkin' horseshit," the thug's youthful, ruddy-faced accomplice yelped in agreement.

At that point, barely ten feet away from all three of the sassy participants in the dustup, Longarm stopped and very deliberately slipped his coattail back. The none-too-subtle move revealed the bone-gripped, silver-plated, double-action Colt .44-caliber Lightning. For the moment, it slept benignly in the well-oiled cross-draw holster resting on Longarm's left side.

"That 'ere fancy pistol s'posed to skeer me?" the brawny tough snapped. He patted the notched, walnut grip of the impressive-looking Schofield. "Hell, I got one even bigger'n yern, jerk-off. This here popper'll put a winder in your stringy, interferin' ass wide enough so's anybody what wants to can see all the way through to all outdoors."

Longarm turned his palms up and forced a friendly, ambiguous smile. "Now look, mister, this gent evidently has a problem with your boy there. Appears as how the lad is guilty of some rather questionable business practices—sugar tits or not."

The thug's head snapped back. "Huh? What the hell'd you just say?"

"I'd like to suggest that this gentleman be allowed to search the kid. If there's no watch, we can all just go our separate ways and forget about the entire unfortunate episode. If he finds his watch, then we might want to think about havin' this filthy-mouthed youngster taken into custody by local authorities and perhaps admitted to the Colorado State Reformatory for Boys. A year of disciplined living, a taste or two of a come-to-Jesus meetin' now and then, might do him a world of good."

The filthy-faced waif's reaction was immediate and loud. "Damnation, Hogue, ignore the lanky son of a bitch. Doan wanna be a-goin' to no reformatory. Been in enough of 'em already. 'Member me a-tellin' you 'bout that 'un in St. Louie? Still have nightmares over that 'un. Now, git me loose a this asshole and let's get the hell outta here."

As his efforts didn't appear to be going anywhere, Longarm scratched an ear and offered up another choice. "Well, then, how 'bout this, young feller? How 'bout you just give this gent's watch back and you two can go on your merry way like nothin' ever happened. No reason for lockin' horns and possible gunplay over a theft that never occurred."

More confused than ever by the unexpected turn of events, the bulky brute with the pistol swayed back and forth like an inquisitive Wyoming grizzly bear trying to check out events on the other side of a tree.

Much to Longarm's dismay, for about a tense second, the creature's hand crept toward the grip of the Schofield pistol. But then he appeared to reconsider just short of grabbing at the weapon, and dropped the pawlike appendage back down to his waist again. Nervous fingers played with the hem of his ragged, filth-encrusted coat.

"Dude ain't a-searchin' nobody," Hogue growled. "Dude's gonna turn my friend Ernest loose and right damned quick, or I'm gonna be forced to hurt somebody. Me'n Ernest is a-gettin' the hell away from here, even if I have to kill everbody in sight."

Longarm shook his head. "Well, now, we can't have any of that kinda thing. And in spite of your threats, I don't think this gent's inclined to do what you've suggested, Mr. Hogue. Comes right down to the nut cuttin', can't say as how I blame him. If the loss by theft of my gold retirement watch was in question, I know *I* sure as hell wouldn't turn the boy loose."

The bent-nosed Hogue shot a wicked glance at the natty gent, then at his own red-faced, ear-pinched accomplice. "Damn the fuckin' watch. Gotta let Ernest go, mister. Like I said, doan wanna kill nobody, but I'll sure as hell do'er if'n you doan unfinger that ear and be right damned quick about it."

Longarm shook his head. "Now you don't really mean that stuff 'bout killin' folks, Hogue. No reason to go threat-enin' us with murder and such. Besides, I'm a deputy U.S. marshal, and if you should manage, by some kind of God-sent miracle, to rub out the feller holdin' your friend by the ear and then get me, there'll be so many of my badge-carryin', armed-to-the-teeth compadres up your big ass, you're gonna wish you'd never been born."

"He's a lyin' dog, Hogue," the kid screeched. "He ain't no fuckin' law. Where's his badge? You see one? Go on an' kill 'em both and let's get the hell outta here. Head on down the trail."

Eerily, and all of a sudden, all the sound seemed to get sucked out of the entire world. The raised area of the railroad platform abruptly got quieter than the bottom of a fresh-dug grave at midnight. For about a second, Longarm thought he'd gone deaf. The few remaining travelers still occupying the spot noiselessly scuttled to the nearest exit door, or ducked for cover behind anything available. Any discussion of what to do about the situation had abruptly come to a death-dealing end.

In a single fleeting instant, Longarm locked onto the slitted glaring eyes of the bearlike Hogue. All it took was that one glance for the lawman to know, in the bottom of his being, that the man he'd confronted had every intention of taking the rowdy dispute to its absolute limit and going down with a smoking pistol in his hand.

Under his breath, Longarm muttered, "Shit." Much louder, he called out, "Now, don't do it, Hogue. Think about your precarious position here, man. No point in carryin' this argument any farther. Better to die in bed from chills and fever than here at the end of a smoking pistol. Have the kid give the watch back. Then the two of you can go on your merry way, happy as a pair of pigs in a peach orchard."

For reasons known only to God, Hogue decided to eat the whole weasel, teeth, hair, toenails, and all. To Longarm's absolutely astonished dismay, the possum-brained churnhead grabbed for the massive weapon at his waist.

The Colt Lightning at Longarm's waist came out and up like double-geared lightning. The always careful lawman never wasted time when it came to life-and-death situations. And given that trying to wound a dangerous, obviously criminal opponent in a standup gunfight bordered on the idiotic, as a consequence he didn't aim for an arm or a leg.

The hapless Hogue hadn't even managed to get his weapon's seven-and-a-half-inch barrel cleared of the thick swath of leather around his stout waist when the first of two thunderous, window-rattling blasts delivered massive, .44-slugs into his chest. The initial shot hit him dead center, crushed his breastbone, bored through muscle, sinew, arteries, and veins, and knocked the unfortunate gunny backward into an iron wheel of the baggage cart.

Staggered by the impact of a huge chunk of lead pushed by thirty-eight grains of black powder, Hogue ricocheted off the two-wheeler, then stumbled forward and dropped to his knees. He grabbed at the wound in his chest just as the second bullet punched a hole the size of a man's thumb just above it. The blast knocked him onto his back in a twitching, blood-and-gore-slinging heap.

A churning cloud of acrid-smelling, spent, black-powder smoke wafted from behind Longarm, then rolled across the ten-foot space in front of him on a barely discernible breeze. It engulfed the luggage wagon and his mortally wounded target before quickly dissipating into the cool Colorado air like vented steam from a Baldwin engine.

The distraught kid made a sound like a cat being stomped. He ripped himself out of the natty gent's iron-fingered grip and flew to the fallen Hogue's side. He stood for a second with trembling hands over his ears, as though trying to blot out the sounds he'd just heard. Then he let out another animalistic screech, fell on the dead man's oozing chest, and wept like the saddest wolf in the great cold and lonely. The kid's noisy weeping simply deepened Longarm's regret for having had to kill a man for what he considered a stupid reason.

The natty gent swept his hat off, pointed a shaking finger at Hogue, then said, "You killed him. Jesus, I can't believe you killed him, Marshal."

Longarm shook his head, then calmly flipped the loading gate of the Colt open and ejected the two empties. He fished fresh rounds from his belt, reloaded, and then reholstered the .44.

"Sure as hell didn't want to do it, mister," Longarm said. "You saw and heard the whole dance. I tried my level best to get him not to pull on me. He wouldn't have any of it. Damned shame really. Hell, I wish he'd a-listened to me. But if I hadn't drilled him dead center, he'd a-killed me and maybe you as well."

The natty gent fanned himself with the hat, patted sweat away from a hairless pate with a clean, white handkerchief, and nodded as though still unable to completely believe what he'd just been a part of. "Well, yes, you did," he muttered as though to himself. "Did indeed. Heard you try to reason with the man. He just wouldn't have any of it. My, oh, my."

Longarm pulled his wallet from an inside coat pocket and flipped it open to the silver-plated, deputy U.S. marshal's badge. He removed the emblem of his office, then carefully pinned the polished, impressive star on a spot on the left lapel of his suit coat. Then, he jammed an unlit nickel cheroot between clenched teeth and waited.

Barely half a minute later, three Trinidad lawmen brandishing their pistols rushed onto the bloody scene. From every clue available to Longarm, the local law enforcement types were scared slap to death. Wide-eyed and trembling all over, they jerked their weapons in the direction of the slightest sound, and appeared on the verge of passing out with every wayward, unexpected movement no matter how benign.

Slumped over the corpse, the kid continued to weep and moan. The constant racket had begun to rub at the raw ends of Longarm's already frayed nerves.

Backed up by a pair of deputies, the tallest of the anxious

group of local lawmen—a scar-faced, mustachioed giant of a man—pointed his weapon at Longarm and yelped, "Hold on now, mister. Keep your hands away from 'at 'ere pistol you're a-wearin'. No sudden moves, you son of a bitch, or we'll blast you to Kingdom Come. Swear to Jesus, we will. Now get to tellin' me just what the hell happened here."

As though performing the task underwater, Longarm picked the badge off his chest and held it above his head so no one on the railroad loading dock could possibly miss it.

"Careful there, boys, careful now. I'm Deputy U.S. Marshal Custis Long workin' out of the First District Federal Court in Denver. No need for a show of weapons at this juncture. Shootin's over," he said, and waved the star and waved his wallet.

The tall deputy eased his way toward Longarm. He acted like a man who'd just discovered a western diamondback rattlesnake the size of the barrel from a three-pound Napoleon cannon on the ground in front of him. He snatched the badge and identification out of Longarm's hands, then stalked back to the perceived safety and company of his companions.

For some seconds, Longarm chewed his stogie and watched as the men heatedly consulted amongst themselves, then finally appeared to come to some sort of agreeable decision. The tall deputy holstered his pistol, ambled back over, and returned Longarm's star and identification wallet. Then he held out his hand and said, "Name's Micky Black, Marshal Long. I'm a deputy city marshal here in Trinidad. Hope you understand as how me'n the boys 'uz just bein' careful."

Longarm shook the man's hand, then said, "'Course I understand, Deputy Black. Wouldn't expect it any other way. Do the same myself if confronted with a similar situation. Deadly doin's always require careful consideration far as I'm concerned."

Black glanced at Hogue's blood-soaked body. "Would you mind explainin' what happened here, Marshal Long?"

Longarm ended up taking longer to tell the tale of how the lunatic affair had taken place than the actual incident itself had taken. He eventually waved the natty gent over, and had him recount the events surrounding the shooting as he'd witnessed them. Everyone appeared satisfied with their descriptions of the shooting until City Marshal Mason Dobbs showed up. Then the whole dance started all over again.

After nearly an hour of repeating the entire blood-soaked tale at least three times, Longarm saw his southbound Atchison, Topeka, and Santa Fe connection pull up in a cloud of chugging steam and screeching brakes.

Carrying Longarm's possibles bag and saddle, Marshal Dobbs followed the Denver-based lawman onto the train. "Gonna have to provide me with a written deposition of this sad event, Long. Best thing all 'round for everyone involved. Mind now, I ain't a-questionin' the necessity of what you done, but I'd feel better 'bout the whole situation with that paper in hand. Hope you understand."

"Don't worry, Dobbs. I'll have a notarized affidavit back to you just as soon as I have time to sit down and write it up," Longarm said, and dropped his rifle, rain slicker, and bedroll on another well-worn bench in another day coach. He turned and faced Dobbs before adding, "But I hope you understand, that happy event might be a few days down the road, maybe weeks. I'm on special assignment and have to get to Pecos, Texas, as quickly as possible. Sorry 'bout leavin' this mess for you to clean up, but my response to Hogue's threat could not have been otherwise."

Dobbs nodded and offered his hand. Longarm reluctantly shook it, then flopped into his new seat.

"Understand completely, Marshal Long," Dobbs said. "We all have our assigned responsibilities." He turned and started for the coach's doorway. Over his shoulder, he added, "Please don't forget."

Mere seconds after the departure of Trinidad's city marshal, the train jerked to life again. Like a giant South American snake just roused from a long nap, it slowly began rolling south. From his perch by the window, Longarm watched as Mason Dobbs pulled the still-weeping kid away from the corpse. He wondered how Hogue and the kid had come to such a pass, figured he'd never know, pulled his hat down over his eyes, and immediately fell asleep.

Chapter 6

Two days later, Longarm shifted uncomfortably on a rock-hard, unpadded bench in the Conklin Brothers stage line's waiting room in Toya, Texas. The narrow-gauge railway's terminal town would soon connect with advancing Texas and Pacific construction all the way to Fort Worth in the east. In the meantime, section gangs and all their support structures had turned the treeless, rolling landscape surrounding Toya into a bustling community of nearly a thousand audacious, stalwart inhabitants.

Several impressive structures had risen from the bleak countryside since Longarm's last hurried trip through the area. Most elegant of the edifices was a two-story, red-brick, white-colonnaded structure that contained a bank, the local post office, and telegraph—all on the first floor—along with a growing Masonic lodge and branch of the Eastern Star on the second.

A new hotel, mercantile, drugstore, barbershop, and thriving saloon made up the bulk of other recently erected buildings. Here and there, a number of small, busy cafés of various sorts dotted the landscape as well.

The main thoroughfare was broad, level, uncluttered,

and well maintained. Horse manure barely had time to draw flies before being shoveled up and hauled away by a diligent, uniformed city employee who pushed a rolling, covered steel barrel. The residents of Toya thought of themselves as quite the cosmopolitan lot. Erroneously, of course, but they thought it anyway.

None of these momentous strides in civilization's relentless advance meant much to Longarm at that exact moment. In fact, he'd hardly taken the slightest notice of all the hustle and bustle in an area once reserved for rattlesnakes, tarantulas, wolves, and scorpions.

He had arrived in El Paso late the previous evening and spent the better part of a miserable layover night in a hotel there before arriving in Toya on the narrow-gauge flyer. The squirming lawman would forever after use the term *hotel* sneeringly when describing those rough lodgings because, in truth, the coarse inn barely passed as a flophouse for itinerants of the most questionable sort. A mattress full of insanely aggressive bedbugs had damn near chewed his rail-weary ass right down to the bone before he'd managed to wake up and abandon the grubby room for a spot atop a haystack in a nearby livery's only empty stall.

First thing that morning, before catching the train, he had submitted himself to a skin-singeing cleansing. The bathwater was laced with dissolved borax and lye soap. This ass-blistering remedy was followed with a liberal application of apple-cider vinegar. The combined treatments had gone a long way to alleviating the mass of itchy welts that now decorated his still-irritated rump. But bedbug bites usually had to work themselves out over time, and Longarm was still feeling the consequences of an assault unlike any he could bring to memory, as he fidgeted back and forth on what he had deemed as the Conklin Brothers' wooden instrument of torture.

The fact that he smelled a hell of a lot better than usual didn't matter a great deal to the struggling lawman either. The climes of central Texas, which were much warmer than Denver, had stripped the heavy shearling coat from his body. It now lay at his feet like something about as useful as a boat anchor, and his inflamed backside had once again begun to itch like the very dickens.

While he was the only occupant of the stage line's waiting room at the time, Longarm entertained no desire to violate established decorum by standing to scratch his ass like a flea-ridden dog. A female clerk, working the ticket window, sat staring at him as though she'd never seen an available man before. An inviting smile played across her broad, plain face as she pursed her lips and winked.

Shit, he thought, *there are just some things a gentleman doesn't do—like going at your ass while a strange woman watches.* Eventually, though, the insect-induced irritation could no longer be ignored. He stood, stomped around the room a bit as though trying to knock the dust off his boots, pulled at his pants as discreetly as possible, then headed for someplace outside. He needed to be away from his smiling audience—in a private area where serious, soul-satisfying scratching could ensue.

As he jerked the ticket office's door open, the most astonishing woman he'd seen in years swept across the rough threshold, nodded, and smiled. She was tall, stately, dressed in an elegant, close-fitting, fawn-colored traveling outfit and jaunty, short-brimmed, palm-leaf sombrero, and her golden tresses cascaded from beneath the hat and pooled onto regally held shoulders.

No detectable rouge, powder, or makeup of any kind appeared to have been applied to an unblemished face highlighted by natural, ruby-red lips. A shock of frilly white lace at the woman's throat appeared to frame her

49

splendid countenance as though it were a portrait painted by a long-dead Italian artist who specialized in heart-stopping renditions of honey-haired angels come to earth.

Ever the courteous cavalier, Longarm stepped aside and held the door open with one foot. He snapped to attention, removed his Stetson, and offered a well-executed, graceful, chivalrous bow.

The woman's turquoise-colored gaze, shadowed by long, pale, near-white lashes, quickly scanned him from head to foot, then back again. The striking lady took two more steps, stopped, and made quite a deliberate show of removing a pair of leather riding gloves.

She pursed a set of bow-tie lips, and then said, "Why, thank you, sir. Please be assured that such freely offered gallantry in this most primitive and out-of-the-way place is much appreciated."

The voice was velvety and Southern to the core. The sounds that dripped from her crimson lips were the audible embodiment of soft moonlight falling through magnolia blossoms, mint juleps on the veranda, and vast cotton fields surrounding the colonnaded, family manse.

Longarm flashed his most winning, toothy smile. In that very instant, the inflamed bites on his itchy posterior were totally forgotten. "You are most welcome, ma'am. I'm certain any man of proper upbringing and background would be obliged to conduct himself in exactly the same manner."

Her astonishing, bluish green eyes deepened in color and appeared to sparkle. Ebony pupils widened. "Ah, yes. Well, perhaps, sir. Perhaps. But there's the problem, you see. I've discovered it's something of a distinct rarity to find men *of proper upbringing and background* since my arrival in this rude, godforsaken country. Given that I detect something of a Southern upbringing in your voice, I can well understand why you, of all men, would be the exception to my admittedly casual observations."

Longarm's gaze briefly darted past the astonishing woman to a mountainous pile of luggage stacked on the boardwalk outside. The beautifully tanned set of matched leather bags sported polished brass buckles and silver-plated locks.

He flicked a finger toward the mound of various-sized cases and said, "Yours?"

The woman slanted a lash-fluttering glance toward the stack of gear, before fanning herself with the gloves and saying, "Yes, I must admit they are *all* mine. Each and every one. Had I known transport of such a load would prove so problematic, I think most of it would have been left behind in Georgia."

"I'd be most happy to bring them inside for you," Longarm said, and snugged the Stetson back down on his head.

"How very kind of you to offer your assistance, sir. I do truly appreciate it, but that won't be necessary. I'm here this morning to catch the next departing coach to Pecos. It is my understanding that fortunate event should take place within the hour. As a consequence, in a very short time, the bags would just have to be moved back outside again for loading onto the stage."

News of the prospect of pleasant, and insanely beautiful, companionship for the two-to-three-hour trip to Pecos brought an abbreviated but carefully controlled smile to Longarm's lips. "Well, then, it appears we'll be traveling companions, Miss u-h-h-h . . . Didn't get your name, ma'am."

She extended a flawless hand. "Parker. Constance Parker, sir."

Longarm gently took the hand in his, removed his hat

51

again, then bowed long enough to breathe a kiss onto well-manicured fingers. "My great honor to make your acquaintance, Miss Parker," he said. "Deputy U.S. Marshal Custis Long, working out of the Federal District Court in Denver. Your obedient servant, ma'am." He clicked his heels together like a gallant cavalier of olden times.

The recently kissed fingers dropped back to an onyx and pearl cameo locket the size of a twenty-dollar gold piece that dangled from her neck on a braided, gold chain. As Constance Parker fiddled with the impressive piece of jewelry, she gazed into Longarm's eyes and said, "How very chivalrous of you, Marshal Long. Since departing the comforts of my family home in Pike County, Georgia, three weeks ago, I have encountered examples of the crudest forms of manly behavior imaginable. It is most heartening to know that gentlemen of quality and good breeding do still exist here on the wild and woolly frontier."

"Oh, I can assure you there are still a few of us around, Miss Parker. In spite of the best efforts of bad men, bad women, and a distinct scarcity of reasons for gentle conduct, we do exist and are fairly easy to find. You have but to look in the right directions."

Those words had barely passed Longarm's lips when the Pecos stage wheeled up within a few feet of Constance Parker's stack of expensive luggage. Drawn by a well-harnessed hitch of six fine, magnificently sturdy-looking Morgan horses, the coach, manufactured by the Abbot-Downing Company of Concord, New Hampshire, appeared brand-spanking-new. The shiny vehicle was definitely not the run-down mud-wagon version of frontier transportation Longarm had fully expected.

Painted a bright red and trimmed in brilliant yellow, the coach had a flashy, white American eagle decorating its door below a gilded legend that proclaimed U.S. MAIL. The whole shebang was covered with a thin layer of West Texas's finest dust, but even that could not disguise the obvious splendor of its fresh-faced newness.

The glorious coach had barely stopped rolling when, as if by magic, several stock tenders appeared and began calming the animals, seeing to their individual needs, and then changing them out for a fresh team.

Without comment, Longarm and the woman watched as a rough-looking, barrel-bellied fellow in the driver's seat set the brake, twisted leather reins around the wooden handle, then lumbered down from his regal roost atop the leather front boot. He snatched an enormous sugarloaf sombrero from his bearlike head, beat at his grime-covered canvas coat, and sent a billowing cloud of powdery topsoil rolling in all directions.

"Bet I could grow a fine crop a turnips right here on my own belly," the big man said, and then laughed out loud.

He turned and snatched the coach's door open. "Step on down, folks. This here's Toya. That's right, neighbors, Toya. Garden spot of West Texas. You kin catch the narrow-gauge on to El Paso over yonder at the depot." His eager hand assisted a pair of frumpy, tired-looking women with their exit, but he made no move to aid the men, who disembarked and wandered away slapping at their own dust-covered clothing.

A snaggle-toothed smile etched its way across the coachman's heavily mustachioed, friendly face when he glanced over at the office door and realized he had an audience. The gapped smile got even broader when his gaze landed on Constance Parker.

He straightened himself, pulled at his coat lapel, stomped the heavy layer of dust off his boots, then strode to the open doorway. Sombrero in one hand, he pushed sweat-drenched strands of hair away from twinkling eyes with the other and bobbled his head in greeting like an enormous waddling turtle.

"You folks bound for Pecos?" His admiring gaze never left Constance Parker's face.

Custis Long and the woman both nodded. Had Longarm suddenly burst into flames, he doubted the driver would have even noticed. In fact, he thought, the flames from his torchlike body could consume the entire building and this man wouldn't take his eyes off the Parker woman long enough to even blink.

"Well, now, that's mighty fine to know. Mighty fine. 'Pears as how you folks'll likely have the coach all to yore-selves on this trip. Should be a right comfortable, un-crowded trip. I'll check in with the ticket agent just to make sure there ain't no other passengers. Be right back to load yore baggage. This here stack a stuff on the boardwalk yours, miss?"

Constance Parked smiled and nodded. "Yes. I do hope you'll excuse the enormity of the load."

The driver slapped his hat back on. "Oh, don't you worry yourself none, ma'am. Loaded and unloaded enough freight over the years to fill up Palo Duro Canyon. That tiny heap a stuff won't be no trouble a'tall. No, ma'am. No trouble a'tall."

Constance Parker gifted the man with a radiant smile. "Why, thank you, sir. Your assistance and goodwill are greatly appreciated."

"You can call me Val, ma'am. Short for Valentine. François Valentine Devine, that's my given name. 'Course I never cared for that Frenchyfied-soundin' piece of it in the front. My dear sweet mammy give it to me, but I never cared for it nohow. Caused a world a hurt when I 'uz a kid. Or Valentine either, come to think on it. So, folks just call me

Val. 'Less they want the sulfurous hellfire beat out of 'em. Pardon my language, miss. Don't mean to offend."

Constance Parker's smile widened even more. "No offense taken, Mr. Devine."

Valentine Devine's face lit up like a Fourth of July whizbang. He toed the rough boards beneath his enormous feet, then said, "Aw, shucks, ma'am. Ya'll jus' go on ahead an' climb aboard at yore leisure. I'll check in with the ticket agent, get yore goods strapped into the back boot, and we'll be on our way. If you'll excuse me, I'll be back so quick you'll think I wuz a-backin' up. Might be big but I'm fast. My wife, Maria, says I'm so fast I could thread a needle on one a them foot-pumped sewin' machines."

As Devine chuckled at his own joke and nodded his way past them, Longarm said, "Well, there you have it, Miss Parker. You've now met two well-mannered gentlemen in a row this very morning. And way out here in on the backside of nowhere to boot. One of 'em a bit rougher than the other, but a pair of living, breathing gentlemen at the core nonetheless."

When she smiled at his comical observation, he made so bold as to take the lady by the elbow and guide her to a spot on the boardwalk near the rear wheel of the waiting coach.

The stock tenders had worked with amazing speed and in a matter of minutes had had the empty, idle coach attached to a rested, eager team of horseflesh and readied for its return run to Pecos.

The newly arrived horses in the hitch impatiently stamped their feet and flicked their tails about in a never-ending effort to shoo pesky, thumb-sized flies away from quivering flesh. The musical rattle of metal buckles, trace chains, and snaps against wooden singletrees and leather resulted from the team's continuous, ever-shifting, head-shaking movements.

While it was a pleasant and rather quiet day, Toya's main street bustled with foot traffic. Men, women, and even a few children darted around the couple on the boardwalk. Spring wagons, buckboards, heavy drays, and a fancy cabriolet or two passed up and down the lively thoroughfare adding to the growing town's general congestion and hubbub.

With no warning whatever, a series of rapid, thunderous gunshots split the air. Catlike, and responding with nothing more than the lifesaving instincts derived from years of experience, Longarm sprang into action.

He grabbed Constance Parker and roughly shoved her against the stage depot's board-and-batten wall. At almost the same instant, he brought the Colt on his left hip into play and covered her body by pressing against her with his own.

From the corner of one eye, he spotted a pair of drunken, rubber-legged cowboys exiting the Sunset Saloon a few doors down from the stage office. Pistols and whiskey bottles firmly in hand, the drunken amigos staggered toward their rough, skittish cow ponies and continued to shoot holes into an empty, cloudless sky.

Constance Parker clung to her protector like a frightened child. She buried her face against Longarm's shoulder and pulled him close. He could feel her warm, moist breath on his neck. The aroma of gardenia-scented perfume and the heavy musk of her sex filled his nostrils. Her clinging became more ardent as the boisterous pistol fire continued unabated.

She pressed her wonderfully rounded, lush, female body to his. Like ripe, recently harvested melons, her young, erect breasts pushed against his chest. In no time at all, the gigantic soldier of love between Longarm's legs came to rigid attention and began to respond in spite of the possible danger threatening them. After another round of deafening gunshots, the trembling girl almost appeared determined to press herself through Longarm's clothing and become a part of him.

Growing closer, the senseless and indiscriminate gunfire sounded like cannons going off as it ricocheted from glass windows in the buildings along Main Street and cracked east and west at the same time. The Conklin Brothers' fresh team of Morgans jerked, whinnied, and sidestepped in an effort to get away from the sound of each indiscriminate, thunderous explosion. The dismayed stock tenders had their hands full trying to control the frightened animals.

Much to Miss Parker's obvious relief, in a matter of seconds, the pair of rowdy brush poppers had somehow gotten themselves mounted. They raged off down the now nearly empty thoroughfare toward the west side of town, guns still blazing.

Wild-eyed, Valentine Devine's team of animals continued to crow-hop, skitter, whinny, and shake their heads at the noise as the cowboys raced past. But with the devoted attention of the stock tenders, they held their place.

Longarm had pushed back and started to move away from Constance Parker when the drunker-than-hoedown-fiddlers duo of leather pounders twirled their mounts about like four-legged cyclones and made a second noisy run back toward the east. He stepped up against the girl again, and she welcomed the safety of the shelter he offered.

After the passage of several more seconds, it appeared the inebriated waddies had managed to fire off all their live rounds. They holstered their empty pistols and resorted to little more than the kind of meaningless hat-waving, whooping, and hollering typical of men who wouldn't remember a single second of that day's events when the following morning arrived. Longarm knew the red-eyed buckaroos would likely brag about hoorahin' the town, but remember little if any of the experience.

Once the noise died down, storekeepers, shoppers, bank customers, and gawkers of every stripe stepped from the doorways of businesses all up and down the thoroughfare on both sides of the street. They pointed, commiserated with one another, and railed at the addle-headed inconvenience of it all.

Chapter 7

As a semblance of quiet once again descended on the street, Longarm gazed down into Constance Parker's shocked face, then eased backward a step. For the first time in years, he felt just a bit embarrassed by his actions, in spite of the fact that he had nothing to be embarrassed about. The object of his protective efforts watched wide-eyed as he holstered his pistol. And he took notice when, for the briefest of seconds, her gaze flicked across his crotch, then away and into the street.

"Appears the danger, if there ever really was any, has passed, miss," he mumbled. "Please forgive my hasty impertinence with your person. Must admit, however, that I do tend to get a bit nervy when folks start firing weapons anywhere nearby. It's an unfortunate result of past experience with firearms."

The red-faced girl ripped the palm-leaf sombrero off and then energetically fanned herself with her gloves. An impish smile crept across quivering lips. "That's quite all right, Marshal Long. Personally, I must confess that, while totally unaccustomed to such manly mischief, the whole experience was most stimulating to the blood." She blotted her damp forehead on the sleeve of her dress, then resorted to fanning the hat for a larger, more effective way of cooling her flushed face.

"Men and boys out this way can be rowdy, miss. It's the result of a hard way a livin'."

"Well, I think I can safely say that, beyond any shadow of a doubt and on the whole, the entire incident was most invigorating. As a matter of plain fact, it is the first time in recent memory that any man has seen fit to throw himself upon me, for the view of anyone passing in the thoroughfare, while endeavoring to save my life by offering up his own. I am not sure I know how to respond to such courageous, freely offered gallantry."

Longarm smiled. "I am your obedient servant, ma'am."

In a display of bold confidence, she reached out and touched his arm. The caress was warm, affectionate, and lingered. "Thank you, sir. My most heartfelt thanks. Perhaps I will someday be able to repay your display of audacious concern."

Longarm nodded, then said, "Well, now that the activity appears to have settled down a bit, I think you can safely wait here in the overhang's shade until your luggage is loaded, Miss Parker."

She gazed absently at the street as it began to refill with inquisitive people. "Yes."

"Mite oppressive inside the ticket office. This spot should, at the very least, be a bit cooler. Seems right pleasant out here where the air is moving around some. Good view of all the comings and goings as well—including any cowboy hoo-hah. But hopefully, we won't have any more drunken displays like the one you just had to suffer through. Now, if you'll excuse me, I've luggage of my own to load."

Longarm tipped his snuff brown Stetson, and within a few minutes had placed all his goods inside the Concord's

60

roomy rear boot. His ubiquitous ball-buster McClellan saddle, with attached canteen, saddlebags, bedroll, and possibles bag, made for a fairly neat, easily movable package when all was properly hitched, tied, and fastened to the various brass fittings located all over the army surplus rig. The Winchester hunting rifle, wrapped in his shearling coat, went on the coach's front-facing seat near the spot where he planned to sit. The rifle was carefully arranged for quick and deadly access should it be needed.

As he finished up with his chores, the sweating lawman noticed Constance Parker still fanning her now-flushed face with the hat she'd removed earlier. He stepped to her side, tipped his own hat again, then said, "It is somewhat warmer out here than I'd expected, Miss Parker. I'm fairly certain you'll be more comfortable once we're aboard and get moving. In the meantime, there's a barrel of fresh, cool water inside. It would be my pleasure to bring you a cup if you'd like one."

She dabbed at her eyes with a tiny handkerchief. "Why, yes, I do declare, Marshal Long. Most thoughtful of you to offer. You are entirely correct in your assessment of the weather. I can say without qualification, it is much warmer this morning than I would have ever expected. I feel as though I may have overdressed for such weather. A bit of liquid refreshment would be most appreciated."

About the time the thirsty lady had finished her drink, Valentine Devine reappeared carrying a locked and very official-looking U.S. Mail pouch. He pitched the bag into the front boot, then turned to his only passengers, swept his sombrero off again, and extended a massive paw of a hand that had two joints of the little finger missing.

"Well, miss," he said, "think we're all primed and ready to blow outta Toya and hit the trail. If you'll just come this way, it would be my great honor to help you climb aboard this fine

61

new Concord coach the company recently put into service." As though telling a secret, he added, "It's actually the private coach of one of the Conklin brothers, but the one we generally use for this run busted an axle and it ain't been fixed yet."

With that out of the way, Devine gently clasped the arm Constance Parker offered and escorted her the few remaining steps to the coach. To Longarm's concealed amusement, the burly driver made quite a show of courtly good conduct in his fussy assistance of the woman as she boarded. *Perhaps we've done our part in dispelling the lady's unfortunate attitude about the men of the West,* he thought. *Good morning's work for both of us.*

Once his beautiful passenger was properly seated, and fussed over, according to what appeared to be a set of self-imposed and somewhat exacting standards, Devine turned to Longarm and said, "Jus' go right on and hop in, mister. Soon's you get settled, we'll be on our way."

Longarm glanced in at Constance Parker, then motioned Devine to one side. He guided the rather hesitant man several steps in the direction of the driver's box. Then he stopped and slanted a quick look around to make sure no one passing on the boardwalk might be listening in. Then he said, "Mind if I ask you what I consider a rather important question, Mr. Devine?"

A look of puzzlement and concern settled on Devine's open-faced, cherry-cheeked countenance. "Depends on what kinda question you've got in mind, mister."

Longarm leaned closer. Under his breath and in an affected, conspiratorial-sounding voice, he said, "Hear tell there's been some trouble recently between here and Pecos, what with mail robberies and suchlike on this run. Even heard tell as how an employee of the line got his sad self killed just a few weeks past. Got me to wonderin' as to why you don't have a shotgun guard riding up top beside you."

"Well, why're you askin'?"

Longarm reached inside his jacket, pulled his wallet, and flipped it open to the silver deputy U.S. marshal's badge inside. Devine's eyes popped open to the size of saucers.

"Name's Custis Long, Mr. Devine. Truth is," he said, "my primary reason for being here is to investigate the recent mail thefts perpetrated against the Conklin Brothers line. But more importantly, right now anyway, I'm just a little bit concerned about the lady's safety."

Devine's confused look vanished and the friendly smile returned. "Oh, that. Well, there's no need to worry yerself none, Marshal Long. She's safe as bein' in God's back pocket when I'm a drivin'."

"That a fact?"

"Oh, yeah. Now, sure enough, they's been a holdup here and there over the past couple a months. Cain't very well avoid 'em in places as wild as this part a Texas. Truth is, I've seen robberies of one kind or another with every stage line I've ever worked. And believe me when I tell you, I've worked damn near all of 'em one time or t'other. None of the roadside holdups we've had 'round these parts, till recently anyways, really amounted to much."

"How's that?"

"Well, them *bandidos* never have molested any of the passengers. An' besides, we don't carry no strongboxes full a gold, or bank bags full a money, or anything like that on our coaches. Leastways, not very often. 'Bout the only thing we carry of any importance is these mail pouches, ya see. But then, it is true, somebody did go an' kill the hell outta a driver name a Harley Beckwith a few weeks back for the pouch."

"So I've been told. Sad to hear about the poor man's departure from this life."

"Yeah. Guess some would say it was right sad. Mighty

odd, too. 'Course, a passenger on that same run tole me ole Harley mighta contributed more'n a little bit to his own demise, if you get my meanin'."

"Not sure I do get your meaning, Mr. Devine."

Devine's head jerked around as though he, too, feared someone might be listening. Then he said, "Well, ya see, Ole Harley wasn't the most genial sort. Have no doubt he wuz the kinda feller prone to hump up, pull a pistol, and get to fightin' back for little or no reason a'tall."

"In other words, a thickheaded sort?"

"Well, let's jus' put it this way. With Harley, you could explain somethin' to 'im, but you couldn't understand it for 'im. If you git my meanin'?"

"Clear as a glass of fresh rainwater."

"Passenger I talked with who witnessed the ugly event said Ole Harley got into a cuss fight with one a them bandits when they stopped him and demanded the mail pouch. Said he warn't a-gonna give it up. Then he went to work with his weapon. Even got off the first shot or two, as I'm told. But he missed and one a them bandits didn't."

"That's a shame."

"Yeah, well, Harley never could hit his own ass with a set of deer antlers and five free jabs. Bet I tole that stupid son of a bitch ten times he should replace that old cap'n'-ball .44 Colt he carried. Wonder the thing even fired. But he were attached to it 'cause of him a-carryin' it at the Battle of Chickamauga and all. Stupid as hell if'n you ask me. Shoulda jus' handed the mail sack over and finished the trip on to Pecos. Don't get me wrong. U.S. mail's important and all, for certain sure. But, hell, it ain't worth dyin' over."

"So, you're not overly concerned with the prospect of us being robbed on this run?"

"Oh, hell, no. *Bandido* sonsa bitches stop me, I'll jus'

throw that ole mail pouch at 'em an' keep on a-humpin' it for home."

"Robberies take place around the same spot along the road to Pecos, or have the bandits been varying their tactics?"

Devine scratched his stubble-covered chin. "Well, now, you know, come to think on it, all three of them holdups, so far as I know about, took place in a spot not far from Turkey Rock."

Longarm cast a gaze down the road running east. "How far out is Turkey Rock, Mr. Devine?"

"Oh, 'bout two miles t'other side of the Salt Draw. Road kinda narrows down between a right strange outcroppin' of boulders and rocks that God probably put there just to vex travelin' men. Never have been able to figure out why them stage line engineer fellers ran the damned road right through the middle of that particular spot. Only thang ever made any sense to me was the possibility that one o' them surveyors done it 'cause he figured folks as was jus' a-travelin' through would like the scenery. Hell, they coulda just as easily 've gone around. 'Course, I 'spose that woulda added another two to four miles onto the trip, though. Cost more money. That kinda thang."

Longarm pulled out a nickel cheroot. Fired the smoke to life, then looked thoughtful as he pitched the dead match into the street. "Tell you what, Val," he said. "Before you get to the Salt Draw, I'll climb up top with you. Ride shot-gun on into Pecos. How's that sound?"

Devine offered up a shrug. "Fine by me, Marshal. Does get kinda lonesome up there on the box after a spell. Ain't never minded company while I work."

Longarm slapped the beefy driver on the shoulder and nodded, "Well, then, that's what we'll do. Bandits try to take you on, we'll give 'em somethin' hot to think about. One other thing. I'd appreciate it if you'd keep my status as a lawman to yourself once we get to Pecos. Think you could do that for me?"

A big grin flashed across Valentine Devine's face and he rubbed his hands together. "Sure, Marshal, whatever you say. Your secret's safe with me. And you know, I always did enjoy surprisin' folks. Most 'specially the kind like them as kilt ole Harley. Bet if'n them thievin' weasels try to have this here coach of mine stand and deliver on this trip, we'll give 'em what fer, won't we?"

"Absolutely. Bit of the ole what-fer never hurt any of the world's no-account, thievin' weasels," Longarm said, then stepped into the coach and pulled the door closed behind him.

Some Concords contained three padded and upholstered benches and were fully capable of transporting up to twenty passengers—three on each bench inside the coach and as many as a dozen more strategically placed on the roof. Valentine Devine's shiny new coach was a somewhat smaller, more opulent, version. It sported tufted leather upholstery, leather curtains for all the windows, oversized lamps on each side of the driver's box, only two seats, and it lacked the center bench.

Longarm took the seat across from Constance Parker. His view of the astonishing girl tended to be much better from that angle. Easier to see into her eyes, he thought. He glanced out the window at Valentine Devine, then said, "Let 'em buck, Val. And don't forget to stop at the Salt Draw."

The shiny, new Concord sagged under Devine's massive weight as he climbed into the driver's seat and fussily got himself settled. Longarm heard the brake lever snap back down as it was released, and the rattle of the reins as Devine slapped them over the backs of his anxious team.

Then Devine shouted, "Buck, Blackie, Bess." The coach jerked forward. Movement was slow at first, but in a matter of seconds, the near-empty coach was plowing along the rough road outside Toya and headed east for the rough-and-tumble town of Pecos like the back wheels were afire. Pecos and whatever deadly unknowns awaited, or might be hidden along the primitive West Texas road near Turkey Rock, lay somewhere ahead.

Chapter 8

Once the swaying stage appeared to have leveled into an easy, comfortable rhythm, Longarm pulled a nickel cheroot from his coat pocket. He motioned toward Constance Parker with the stogie. "Mind if I smoke, ma'am?"

"Please do go right ahead, Marshal Long. Unlike many women, I've always favored the smell. Tends to remind me of my father. He loved a good cigar."

Longarm fired the square-cut cheroot, then flicked the dead match out the window. He welcomed a lungful of the soothing tobacco, puffed a ring toward the coach's ceiling, then said, "Given our recent closeness, Miss Parker, I see no need for us to remain so formal. I would be most pleased if you would call me Custis. Or by my nickname, Longarm, if you prefer."

She gifted him with a quick, coquettish smile. "Only if you'll call me Constance, Custis."

"Done. Now, Constance, what brings a lady of your obvious tender upbringing and background all the way out to the backside of a hellish Texas?"

For several seconds, she gazed out the window at the barren, treeless landscape as it drifted past. "My uncle, Custis.

My mother's brother sent for me. He owns one of the largest grocery, mercantile, and feed operations in the entire area around Pecos."

"And he needs a beautiful, educated young woman to help with the books?"

She dropped her gloves into the hat lying on the seat. "Well, not exactly. From the correspondence I've received, Uncle Frank evidently suffers from a weak heart. And perhaps a number of other physical maladies as well. Mother always said he was the sickliest of her seven brothers."

"Seven brothers. My, oh, my. Must've been a sizable family?"

"Yes. Mother had ten sisters as well."

"Good God. Eighteen children. Your grandmother must've been one helluva woman. Sounds like she spent most of her life carrying a child."

"Yes. Cecilia Boudreau Clegg was indeed, as you so aptly put it, quite a woman. Unfortunately, she passed away several years ago."

"Sorry to hear it."

"Uncle Frank and my mother were the youngest of the clan. Always close. He could have sent for any of his numerous nephews or nieces to come out and assist with his business. I attribute my good fortune to his love for my mother."

"Ah. I hope you will forgive the forwardness of what I'm about to say, Constance. But given your obvious beauty, it tends to make a man wonder why you're not married and under the care and keeping of a devoted husband."

She tilted her head and arched an eyebrow. "Perhaps that's because I've never cared to be 'under the care and keeping of a devoted husband,' Marshal Long."

Longarm gauged the soft-gloved sting of her words, then took another puff on the cheroot. "While I have the greatest respect for such forward-thinking attitudes, Constance, you must admit that ours is a difficult world for unattached women—young or old. In point of actual fact, single, unescorted young women of refinement are a rarity in this wild and wicked place."

"That is precisely why I'm on my way to Pecos, Custis. My uncle's offer appears an excellent opportunity for an ambitious young woman like me to get somewhere in a world created by, for, and about men. His wife, my aunt by marriage, passed some years ago. He's childless. And from what I've been able to ascertain from his letters, he's willing to name me as beneficiary to all his worldly goods once God sees fit to call him home. All I have to do is learn his business, top to bottom."

Longarm arched an eyebrow. "It appears you'll someday make someone a great catch as a wife, Constance Parker. Yes indeed, quite a catch."

After that rather pointed comment, their conversation tapered off to nothing more than a few words exchanged here and there. Mostly, Longarm answered innocuous questions about geography, or the flora and fauna of the region. Constance seemed particularly interested in the aggressiveness of Texas rattlesnakes and the possibility of banditry along the near deserted road.

Their trip had been under way little less than an hour when Valentine Devine reined the coach to a stop, then called down, "Salt Draw's just a mile or so ahead, Marshal. You wanna climb on up and sit with me, best do 'er now."

Longarm grabbed his long-barreled Winchester, excused himself from company he preferred not to leave, and climbed onto the driver's box. Upon squirming himself into a good spot, he noticed a heavy cloth bag of rocks sitting on the seat between him and Devine.

Once settled, Longarm glanced around from his grand, high perch and said, "Let 'er rip, Val." Then he grabbed a rock from the bag and pitched it at the enormous, muscular haunch of the nearest Morgan.

Within a matter of minutes, the snorting team waded across an ankle-deep trickle of brackish, scum-covered water. "Salt Draw ain't much of a river, is she?" Longarm observed.

Devine flicked his reins and yelped, "Blacky, Buck, Bess." Then, from the corner of his tooth-poor mouth, he said, "Nope, she ain't much more'n a tricklin' ditch right now, that's for sure. 'Bout three days a year, though, this barely movin' dribble turns into a torrent that'd scare the holy bejabbers outta Noah. Jus' depends on whether we get any rain round these parts. Rare, but it does happen. Seems like it don't take but about a teacup full to flood ever'thang for miles and miles. 'Course it's been pretty dry of recent."

Gently rocking on three-inch-wide strips of thick leather called thoroughbraces, the fancy new Concord effortlessly cruised along on wheels six inches deep in a set of well-used, dust-filled, hardpan ruts. Like a double-gashed ribbon of scabbed-over flesh, the stage road spooled out in front of them and faded into the vastness of the rolling, parched-grass hills of West Texas. Twenty miles to the south, the Barilla Mountains rose from the horizon like growing storm clouds. Civilization lay somewhere in the unseeable east.

Longarm gazed into the hazy, heat-curtained distance and pointed. Ahead, a barely discernible, flint-colored bump in the great sea of brown grew from the earth. "Is that Turkey Rock we're comin' on up yonder?"

Devine nodded. "Yep. Closer we get to that stack a pebbles, the easier it'll be to understand what I wuz a-tellin' you back in Toya. Never really gave the thing much thought before, but she's sure 'nuff a serious choke point that's ideal for road agents and the like."

Nearly an hour later, Longarm eyeballed Turkey Rock

from one end to the other. The jagged pile of stones appeared to have been pushed up from the earth's molten core by some vengeful spirit bent on playing tricks on gullible men. Jutting heavenward out of the earth for several hundred feet, the mile-wide shelf of Turkey Rock's reddish brown slate appeared to have split down the middle leaving a neat, roofless, tunnel-like passage through to the eastern side. Stunted hackberry trees, several varieties of dwarf holly bushes, and massive tufts of dried grass dotted an otherwise barren, featureless landscape around the impressive landmark.

The coach was still a quarter of a mile from the well-known local landmark when Longarm's fingers tightened on the checkered grip of the Winchester. He jabbed Devine in the ribs with his elbow and pointed, then levered a fresh shell into the rifle's receiver.

Up ahead, twinkling sunlight reflected off drawn pistols. Riders. Two men. Masked. One stationed on either side of the road, just before it disappeared into the stone outcropping's shaded, narrow passage—a tight and obviously dangerous channel leading to its eastern extremity and safety.

Longarm grabbed a handful of rocks from the bag and peppered the team's sweating flanks. "Don't stop, Val," he shouted. "Hell, don't even slow down. Turn 'em loose and run 'em like six-legged bobcats."

Devine's face split into a wide grin. His thick forearms came up, then quickly dropped. The reins slapped the backsides of every long-limbed Morgan in the hitch. The muscular team's heads dropped several inches and their strides lengthened from a steady, energy-saving lope into an easy, comfortable run.

Longarm leaned over the side of the coach and yelled, "Constance. Get down on the floor."

Her face appeared at the window—an odd, inquisitive mask of beauty. She shrugged and showed an upturned palm. "Get down on the floor," he yelled again. "Looks like there's bandits up ahead. We're gonna blow by 'em."

With little time to spare, he turned his attention back to the dangerous business at hand. A little over a hundred yards from the masked desperadoes, Longarm spotted their obvious confusion. He leaned back and chuckled just as the gunman on his left, mounted on a pinto, fired the first shot. The heavy pistol slug nicked the corner of the iron luggage cage, and pinged off into the desert emptiness that closed in behind the coach as it barreled toward danger-filled confrontation.

"Lucky son of a bitch," Longarm yelped, then shouldered his weapon and levered three quick, booming rounds through the Winchester. A deadly accurate series of blasts bounced sharp echoes off Turkey Rock.

The pinto stumbled, then went down in a heap as the coach thundered past the squealing, kicking animal. The animal's rider lay on his side, one leg trapped beneath his wounded mount. He pushed at the saddle with his free foot, but appeared unable to break free.

"Mite lucky myself, I guess," Longarm yelled.

Devine nodded and grinned, but his countenance quickly grew serious again when he jerked his head in the direction of the downed man's accomplice. The second bandit appeared on the verge of regaining his composure.

Longarm took the hint. He leaned over Devine's back. Working the lever as fast as he could, he sent a like number of blistering, attention-getting slugs in the direction of the second gunman. The unpredictable sway and bounce of the coach skewed Longarm's aim and resulted in a poorly delivered series of spray-and-pray blasts that kicked up cyclones of dirt at the feet of the bandit's shiny-coated blood bay. Longarm's piss-poor aim didn't seem to matter. The surprised brigand very quickly decided that hightailing it for the nearest cover was a better option than chancing a stand-your-ground fight with a determined shooter who had no reluctance to respond.

In a cloud of dust and noise, the Conklin Brothers' yellow-wheeled coach hit the jagged entrance of Turkey Rock, and whizzed along the rough road for several hundred yards with no further interference.

Once he'd gotten to his knees and checked behind to make sure they weren't being followed, Longarm called out, "Let's bring 'er to a halt, Val. Need to check on the lady."

Devine eased back on the reins, brought the lumbering stage to a slow, comfortable stop in a nice flat spot, then set the brake.

One eye still glued to the road behind, Longarm hopped down, rifle in hand, and jerked the coach door open.

Like a tightrope walker in a traveling circus, Constance Parker appeared to be trying to balance herself on the tufted leather seat. She looked a disheveled mess. Her hair was askew, the top two buttons of her bodice were open, and her ample breasts heaved as though she was straining to breathe in enough of the dense desert air.

"I had begun to wonder if we would ever slow down, Marshal Long," she said, and pushed sweaty strands of blond hair out of her eyes. Fanning her flushed face with her gloves, she forced a smile and then added, "My goodness, what an invigorating ride."

In spite of himself, Longarm nervously toed at the dirt beneath one foot. "Well, suppose I shoulda warned you that things might get a bit dicey when we stopped back on the other side of the Salt Draw and I climbed up top. Tends to get right bouncy inside one of these contraptions when you have to whip the team up for a hard run. Sorry I didn't get around to saying anything, Constance, but I didn't want you to spend any more time than necessary a-worryin' yourself about what might or might not happen."

She pulled a tiny handkerchief from the sleeve of her dress and dabbed at a stream of sweat along one side of her jaw that trickled down a flawless neck and then into the deep valley between her breasts. "I'm satisfied that you did what you thought best, Custis." Suddenly, an impish grin worked its way across her glorious face. "Besides, that's about the most fun I can remember having since we used to slide down haystacks in my father's fields when I was a child. My goodness gracious."

Longarm threw a quick glance back at the road behind them again, then said, "Well, I'll stay up top with Mr. Devine. It'll give you a chance to straighten yourself up. We should be in Pecos in less than an hour. Wouldn't want you to come off the coach lookin' like you'd just been shot out of a cannon. It might really upset your Uncle Frank."

"Well, you're most thoughtful, Custis. I can assure you that, so long as we don't have another attempted robbery befall us between here and Pecos, all this unwelcome damage to my person will be repaired."

The final leg of the trip from Toya to Pecos passed uneventfully. Longarm maintained his post as shotgun guard on the driver's seat next to Valentine Devine. No threat, not even the hint of a threat, was detected along the mostly deserted stage road after they passed Turkey Rock.

The occasional rider did pass at a distance. Most acknowledged the coach, in one way or another. One cowboy, riding a handsome, prancing sorrel, stood in his stirrups, waved a tall-crowned Stetson, and called Devine's name as the stage sped past.

Now that the trip was almost over, Longarm had to admit to himself that he had genuinely enjoyed Valentine

Devine's genial company. Satisfied with the outcome of the day's events, he looked around at Pecos's bustling principal thoroughfare. It quickly turned into something akin to an anthill some mean-assed kid had stomped on just for the hell of it.

As the coach flew along a hard-packed dirt street, Longarm could see that the sparsely populated fringes of the town quickly changed into a dense, close-packed series of prosperous-looking businesses and store-front buildings. He eyeballed, and mentally noted, the location of wagon yards, hotels, saloons, barbershops, pool halls, a post office, a telegraph office, restaurants, dry-goods stores, tailor shops, dressmakers, a tin shop, and gun dealers.

As Devine guided his team through the rustic burg's rough outer edges and into the principal part of town, Longarm leaned over and said, "Miss Parker's here to visit an uncle, Val. As I understand it, the feller owns a good-sized mercantile outfit. Name of Clegg. Frank Clegg, if memory serves."

Devine shot him an odd, sidelong glance. "Did I hear you right? Frank Clegg? You did say Frank Clegg?"

Longarm nodded, but noted something in Devine's voice that he couldn't quite put a finger on but didn't particularly like. "Yep. Frank Clegg. Thought maybe you could carry her right up to the steps of her uncle's business. Figure that'd make her arrival where she's about to start a new life really special. But now, that's only if it won't cause you any added trouble, Val."

Just past the town's welcome sign, Devine leaned over as close to Longarm as he could get. The burly stagecoach driver nodded, but appeared somewhat distressed by Longarm's request.

In spite of the cacophony of racket rising from the busy street and the six-hitch team of Morgans, Devine was nigh on whispering when he jerked his massive head around, then said, "Would I be right in guessin' the lady ain't heard the sad news 'bout her uncle, Marshal? Mr. Clegg, that is?"

"Sad news? What sad news?"

"Why, he was murdered, Marshal Long. Just a couple a days ago."

"You're bullshittin', ain't you, Val?"

"Oh, no sirree-bob, sir. Horrible doin's that. Someone snuck in and kilt the poor man deader'n a seal-tight of corned beef late one night whilst he was a-sitting at his desk a-doin' books for his business. Walked up and put a blue whistler right through the base of his skull bone. Heard tell it came out his mouth. Some said the whole top a his desk was covered with bloody teeth. Nasty business that killin'. 'Bout as nasty as they come. Seems to me as how Miss Parker done made a helluva long trip just to visit with a dead man."

Chapter 9

Longarm left his Winchester on the seat and climbed down from the driver's box to assist Constance Parker. When the coach door swung open, the Georgia beauty stepped out looking like European royalty. Not a single strand of the astonishing woman's golden tresses appeared out of place. Not one spot of wayward dust remained on her immaculate traveling dress.

Stunned by such an amazing recovery, Longarm nodded, grinned, and did a kind of shuffling dance like an impressionable twelve-year-old. *God Almighty,* he thought, *just nothin' like a beautiful woman to make a grown man feel like a complete, blithering idiot.* Then, because their recent closeness had bred a certain degree of familiarity, for just a moment he allowed himself to wonder what she would look like in bed stark nekkid with her legs spread apart. The image caused him to shake his head, avert his gaze, and stare at the toes of his boots.

With the beaming lawman's studied, gentlemanly assistance, Constance Parker regally descended into the sandy street and stood gazing up at the elaborate sign above the storefront entrance to Clegg's Mercantile, Kitchenware,

Groceries, Dry Goods, and Feed Store. Freshly painted in two-foot-tall bloodred letters, the massive billboard looked fully capable of being seen from just about any spot along the entirety of Pecos's wide, busy, congested, main thoroughfare.

People and animals by the score passed back and forth, raising a cloud of fine dust that hung in the air like a gritty curtain. The ever-increasing hubbub from all the movement made it difficult for people to talk without raising their voices, which further added to the near-riotous clamor and tumult.

For several seconds, Longarm and the striking woman at his side stood in the street without speaking and simply admired the well-kept exterior of the whitewashed clapboard building. After the passage of nearly a minute, Longarm leaned nearer in order to be heard and said, "Fine-lookin' place of business, Constance."

She nodded, and a beaming smile spread across cherry-colored lips. "Yes. Yes, it is, Marshal Long. My Uncle Frank has done himself right proud, I'd say. Right proud indeed."

The bitter pill of Valentine Devine's recently revealed news sat burning on the tip of Longarm's tongue. He moved toward the obviously happy girl to tell her the appalling tale of the mysterious midnight slaughter. But of a sudden, a tall gentleman in an elegant three-piece suit, white shirt, navy cravat, and low-crowned, short-brimmed black hat bustled from the building's double-door entrance. Constance's full attention swerved toward the stranger, who twirled around like an awkward ballet dancer and began to tack a gold-sealed, very official-looking document onto the painted wall between the front door and a large plate-glass display window.

"What's going on here?" the inquisitive girl shouted.

With no hesitation, she immediately stepped away from Longarm's protective side and onto the rugged, six-foot-wide board walkway laid directly atop the ground. "What's the meaning of this, sir?" she called to the well-dressed gent hammering on her uncle's wall.

Tack hammer in hand, the open-faced, mustachioed fellow faced the couple, and immediately became flustered by the golden-haired beauty confronting him. He snatched the spotless hat from his nigh-hairless noggin, danced from foot to foot, then stammered, "U-h-h, well, u-h-h, miss, I have the unfortunate task of, u-h-h, informing the public that Clegg's Mercantile is temporarily closed, at least until such time as, u-h-h, the former owner's beneficiaries can be notified of his untimely recent demise."

As Longarm silently moved to Constance Parker's side again, she snapped, "Untimely recent demise? Uncle Frank has passed? Truly? My word. When did this happen? And who exactly are you, sir?"

The man looked confused. Hammer still clutched in one hand, hat in the other, he swayed for a second like a tree in a stiff wind, but recovered and finally composed himself. "Well, miss," he said. "My good and dear friend Mr. Clegg has fallen victim to foul murder. The dastardly event took place several nights ago. A coward of the first water slipped to his side and assassinated him, as surely as Hell's hot and icicles are cold."

Longarm offered his hand when Constance appeared staggered by the awful news. "My word," she mumbled, and grabbed for his arm. "How awful."

"Exactly. His business has been closed ever since the unhappy episode and his subsequent interment," the stranger continued. "As Mr. Clegg's attorney of record, the document I've just this minute posted on the door is nothing more than legal testament to his passing and proper notification to an inquisitive public as to the procedures I intend to follow in settlement of his rather sizable estate."

Longarm tenderly gripped Constance Parker's elbow. Her voice sounded distant and hollow when she repeated, "Settlement of his estate?"

The man nodded. "Yes, miss. Might I ask if you were acquainted with Mr. Clegg?"

The stunned woman leaned into Longarm's grip. "His niece from Georgia. I'm here in this godforsaken place at my uncle's insistence."

The lawyer's face lit up. "Ah, ha. Is it Miss Constance Parker I have the genuine pleasure of addressing then?"

When she hesitated, Longarm said, "Yes. This lady is Miss Constance Parker."

The lawyer dropped the hammer, clasped his hat in both hands, shifted from foot to foot, and nodded. "Horace Westbrook, attorney at law, at your service, Miss Parker. I've represented your Uncle Frank ever since his arrival here in Pecos. I considered him a close and dear personal friend." He stepped to one side and motioned toward the door. "If you wouldn't mind, could we step inside where it is much quieter and we can talk in private?"

Longarm waved at Valentine Devine and jerked his head to indicate that the driver should continue on to the stage depot. Devine nodded back and yelled, "Conklin's is across the street and all the way out on the eastern edge of town, Marshal. Down past the Orient Hotel and the Gem Saloon. You need me, just send someone. I'll come a-runnin'."

Longarm nodded, then gently urged the shaken girl forward as she trailed behind Lawyer Westbrook and through the now-open doorway of Clegg's Mercantile. Clean, highly polished hardwood floors creaked and groaned beneath their feet.

Typical of such operations, Clegg's general mercantile proved to be a single rectangular high-ceilinged room. Shelves of boxed, or paper-wrapped, dry goods were meticulously arranged behind a twenty-foot-long enclosed counter topped with glass cases all along the left wall.

Groceries, canned staples, pots, pans, and other kitchenware, atop a second glass-fronted countertop, took up the entire opposite side of the room. It fronted a second stack of shelves packed with a variety of necessities, sundries, and a locked weapons' rack filled with assorted shotguns, rifles, and pistols.

A professionally printed sign in the farthest corner indicated that feed goods could be purchased by way of an entry in the alleyway behind the store. A narrow, closed staircase in the opposing corner led to the second floor.

Behind a potbellied stove, sitting dead center in the far end of the room, stacks of men's and women's shoes, boxes of hats, and other ready-made clothing covered the entire back wall. A heavy, metal chandelier hanging in the middle of the room held four large coal-oil lamps.

Any available empty wall space seemed destined for a mounted animal head, or in some cases, the entire beast itself standing on an abbreviated shelf and modeled in an authentic and man-threatening pose—paws up, mouth agape, fangs bared. And in spite of the day's growing warmth, the temperature inside the well-stocked store seemed much cooler and more comfortable than even the shaded, porchlike veranda area on the boardwalk outside.

For the first time, Lawyer Westbrook cast an overtly inquisitive glance in Longarm's direction. "Are you related to the lady, sir? Her husband, perchance?"

Longarm shook his head. "No. We aren't related. I'm simply an interested and concerned friend sworn to look out for Miss Parker's safety and welfare. This is a wild and dangerous part of the country for young women traveling alone, wouldn't you agree, Mr. Westbrook?"

Westbrook scratched his chin. "Yes. Indeed I do, sir. Very dangerous beyond any shadow of a doubt. Why, just recently, the coach you no doubt arrived on has been robbed a number of times. And the passage of but a few weeks has transpired since one of the Conklin Brothers' express guards was murdered. Shameless. Truly shameless."

"I'm completely aware of all that, Mr. Westbrook. But after today's run, such lawless mischief might not happen again. Leastways, not for a spell."

"Ah, well, let us hope so. Senseless, absolutely senseless, if you ask me. And while we can hope for a cessation of such tomfoolery, in my opinion someone else will likely be killed before these criminals can be brought to book for their lawless deeds. I'm sure Miss Parker is most grateful for your protection and guidance under the circumstances, sir."

The loquacious lawyer's words still hung in the air when one of the front doors burst open and banged hard against the inside wall. Longarm, Constance, and Westbrook all snapped startled glances toward the commotion. A gaunt, sallow-faced man, dressed in black from boot sole to hat crown, came gliding in like a ghost arriving to haunt Clegg's mercantile. An all-pervading impression of sullen evil seemed to infuse the air around the man like the kind of rancid body odor a discriminating person notices but doesn't want to acknowledge.

Son of a bitch looks for all the world like an undertaker, Longarm thought, *or maybe a grave robber. Ugly enough to scare the hell out of just about anybody—even in broad daylight. Mother must've fed him with a slingshot when he was a baby. Almost as though death his very own self got up on two legs and walked into the room.*

Constance moved closer to Longarm. He could smell the heavy, sweet scent of magnolias, and feel the heat from her trembling arm against his elbow.

The black-garbed, wraithlike apparition was followed by a pair of heavily armed, wolfish-looking bodyguards. One of the gunnies strode over to the counter on Longarm's right and propped a booted foot atop a small, unopened barrel of pickles. He picked at rotten teeth with a sliver of wood and insolently fingered the butt of a silver-plated, bone-handled Merwin and Hulbert pistol stuffed behind a double-wide leather cartridge belt.

The second gunman took up a post against the door facing as if he intended to block anyone from entering or leaving. The beer-bellied slug spent his time insolently digging at filthy fingernails with a short-bladed Damascus-steel cowboy's boot knife.

From the corner of one eye, Longarm watched as Lawyer Westbrook took a staggering step backward like he'd been slapped hard across the jaw. Color came up in the man's face. He clawed at his throat, as though gagging, and sweat popped out on his brow. The hand grasping his fancy hat quivered.

The skeletal specter in black slithered almost noiselessly across the hardwood floor. He swept a fancy Stetson from his dead-eyed, ashen skull, then woodenly nodded in the general direction of Constance and Longarm in turn. A strange, insincere smirk flashed across his fleshless face, but just as quickly disappeared. Thin, cracked lips peeled away from pointed, yellow, canine teeth in an abbreviated, animalistic snarl.

"Name's Fowler McCabe, folks," he growled. "Happier'n a two-tailed dog to see some new blood in town."

Then, without waiting for acknowledgment of his greeting, or response of any sort, he zeroed his dull, beady, glass-eyed gaze in on Westbrook. McCabe held out the paper that had recently been attached to the wall outside. "Was passin' by and saw this piece a printed bullshit nailed to the wall yonder, Horace. Bein' as how I'm of the opinion that lawyers is the only known enemies of scorpions and insurance companies, I 'uz just a-wonderin' what'n the blue-eyed hell you're up to by postin' such bilge, lawyer man."

Seconds passed. Then time itself seemed to draw to a complete halt. It appeared to Longarm as how everyone in Clegg's Mercantile could suddenly feel the skin-prickling, demoralizing presence of unwelcome death. Slowly, he turned slightly sideways, then rested a hand on the buckle of his gun belt. Murder hung in the air like the smell oozing off a dead animal.

Chapter 10

Horace Westbrook's lips twitched. Beads of sweat rolled down his shiny pate and coursed around piggish ears like tiny rivers. He nodded as though in deference to a superior, but his words belied the uncontrollable responses of his body. In a strong and deliberate voice, the quaking man broke the uncomfortable silence and said, "Up to the business of my former client, the recently departed Mr. Frank Clegg, if you must know, Fowler."

Longarm shifted from one foot to the other, and in doing so revealed the grips of the Colt pistol lying in the cross-draw holster on his left side. Without speaking, he took mental note of the fact that Fowler McCabe displayed all the sinister attributes of one of those men who never blinked. Lifeless, ebony-colored eyes looked like muted lumps of coal. McCabe was a dangerous sort, who did in fact appear more animal-like—or snaky and reptilian—than human.

McCabe's head swiveled on its stalklike neck. His aggressive, commanding stare landed on Longarm. "Don't go an' get all sparky there, *mi amigo*. Any move toward that fancy pistol on your hip could prove right fatal."

Longarm's gaze narrowed. "That a fact."

"Indeed, sir. My boys are widely known to shoot first and worry 'bout the consequences later, if'n you get my drift. Feller there by the pickle barrel's kilt twenty-five men. Wouldn't hesitate to do you just for the sheer fun of it."

In less than a second, Longarm flicked an appraising glance from one of McCabe's henchmen to the other. He quickly assessed the big man who blocked the door as nothing but a fat-gutted slug who would most likely shoot himself in the foot if anything like a requirement for quick and deadly action presented itself.

The bullyboy leaning against the pickle barrel toying with his weapon was another, and somewhat more dangerous, matter altogether. From years of past experience with similar such men, Longarm instantly recognized that of McCabe's two bodyguards, he was indeed the dodgier of the pair.

There was just something about the jagged, lightning-bolt-shaped scar that ran from inside the man's hatband down over a pale, watery, damaged eye and into the scruffy beard decorating his chin that caused an itchy feeling of recollection in the wary lawdog's brain.

It was hard to tell for sure because of a knee-length suit coat, but the darkly ominous-looking McCabe, Longarm noted with some interest, didn't appear armed.

Westbrook held out an upturned, pleading hand. "We want no trouble here, Fowler. No trouble a'tall," he said. "Just having a sociable chat with this young woman and her traveling companion. Niece of Frank Clegg. Just arrived in town on the Toya stage. As executor of Frank's estate, and privy to the contents of his last will and testament, I think I can safely say that I believe this lady is the recently departed Mr. Clegg's sole and only heir."

The lawyer's statement fell on the room like a canister

round fired from a three-pound Civil War Napoleon cannon. From somewhere beyond unimaginable, blood rose up a bony birdlike neck and colored Fowler McCabe's cadaverous face. The dead eyes appeared to sparkle, as though suddenly enhanced by some kind of hellish, brimstone-fueled, internal fire.

"Well, now, that's really somethin' to hear," McCabe grunted, and shifted his fiendish simmering gaze onto Constance Parker.

Westbrook nodded. "Indeed, Fowler, indeed."

McCabe took several silent steps toward Constance. He appeared to float across the floor. Once he'd closed the space and they were within little more than arm's distance of one another, the girl recoiled and pressed even nearer to Longarm as though seeking reassurance.

Longarm patted her arm and whispered, "You're safe, darlin'. Got nothin' to fear."

"By God, if that don't just beat all," McCabe grunted. "No way for you to know it, of course, but 'fore he passed, your uncle mentioned as how something special would soon arrive on the stage. Thought he meant a letter, or somethin' of that nature. Never figured on anything quite like you, miss."

The words wafted across the uncomfortably close expanse between Longarm and McCabe on a cloud of rancid breath odiferous enough to peel paint off a Pennsylvania barn.

Cogs and wheels in Longarm's thinker mechanism all went to spinning at the same time. Images of the man he'd shot at Turkey Rock cropped up. Lookin' for a letter, McCabe had said. As of that moment, Longarm would have bet a hundred dollars McCabe was the driving force behind the stage robberies. Probably no way to prove any connection, though, he thought. Leastways, not at the moment.

"Been tryin' to buy this here place off'n ole Clegg for damn near two years," McCabe continued. "Then, the poor, ignorant son of a bitch goes and gets his stupid self killed deader'n a drowned cat. Now I've got a woman what don't know rock salt from a gin whistle to deal with. Life does have a way of playin' some damned sorry tricks on a man of means and enterprise."

It surprised Longarm when Constance went rigid beside him, then snapped, "My uncle, while many things, sir, could never be described as a son of a bitch. Not even by the likes of you. Frank Clegg was as fine a man as ever lived. And while I may be an inexperienced woman, rudely flung into the rigors of a man's world, I do know the difference between rock salt and a gin whistle. Additionally, if you think for a single instant that you're going to buy me out, you've got another think coming."

McCabe gritted his back teeth so hard, Longarm thought that jaw molars that had been rendered to powder might dribble out the corners of the man's mouth. "Hear me now, woman. I 'uz the first white man to open a mercantile operation of any consequence here in Pecos. That 'uz back when folks 'uz still a-dyin' at the hands of the murderous, bloodthirsty Comanche," McCabe snorted. "These days, my store's the biggest dry goods and grocery operation in town. Biggest west of Fort Worth, as a matter of pure fact. Own a livery, two saloons, a wagon yard, and a hotel. All of 'em right here on Main Street. Damn near half the people in Pecos and for fifty miles in any direction work for me, one way or another. And on top of all that, I'm the most successful rancher in this part of Texas."

Constance jabbed back. "None of that blathering braggadocio matters a whit to me, Mr. McCabe. Not a single whit."

More agitated than before, McCabe waved a pale hand at the contents of Clegg's store. "This little pissant operation is an irritating pimple on my skinny behind. I want to buy it out and close it down. Board up the windows and forget it ever existed. Rid myself of the competition. I'm a fair man, miss. I'll make you a damned fine offer right this instant."

Constance shot a fleeting glance at Westbrook, then glared back at McCabe. "Sir, I traveled here all the way from Pike County, Georgia, to learn how to run this business, and that's exactly what I intend to do. Suffered almost three weeks of near torture so I could stand on this very spot today as a woman with prospects."

McCabe growled like a teased dog, but Constance Parker kept going.

"I put up with bad food, poor accommodations, witless fellow travelers, and an endless stream of wretched, stinking, ill-mannered men. I endured all of that so I could say without qualification, my uncle's store isn't for sale at any price. Not by me at any rate. Not while I'm alive."

McCabe's head dropped. His pointed chin brushed a wizened, caved-in chest. An atavistic, animal-like growl vibrated from somewhere deep inside the man. He brought his angry gaze back up to Constance's face and snarled, "You silly bitch. Jus' like all women, you 'uz born knowin' exactly how to get a rise out of a reasonable man quicker'n a snake can stick out its tongue, weren't you?"

Before Longarm could think fast enough to stop her, Constance Parker took two determined steps in McCabe's direction, then slapped the man so hard his long-dead ancestors, from a hundred years back, must have felt the staggering blow and rolled over in their moldering graves. It looked almost like she brought the open-palmed blow all the way up from the tops of her fancy, high-buttoned leather shoes.

Longarm couldn't help himself and smiled. He wondered if the wax had popped out of McCabe's ears. It looked like she'd knocked McCabe's gizzard loose.

McCabe's gunnies hopped to attention, but appeared confused and uncertain of themselves. They hesitated, and seemed unable to figure out what they should do about the spunky woman's bold action.

McCabe attempted to wave his henchmen off. In spite of that effort, the ruffian standing next to the pickle barrel made a stupid and awkward move for his weapon. Before the clumsy lout could get the pistol limbered up, Longarm had his Colt in play and squeezed off a deafening shot that blew the gun out of the big oaf's hand.

The fancy Merwin and Hulbert weapon, along with a sizable part of the gunny's right thumb, went spinning across the floor like a pair of kid's tops. The badly damaged revolver bounced off a barrel of ax handles and came to rest next to a stack of galvanized water buckets. The ragged chunk of thumb disappeared beneath a rack of ready-made, paper-wrapped lye soap.

The gunny squealed and grabbed a hand that squirted a stream of hot, almost purple blood nigh on three feet into the air. The concussion from the report of Longarm's weapon had everyone else in the room, except the unperturbed lawman, holding their ringing ears and shaking their heads.

For several seconds, a trembling Fowler McCabe appeared as though his head might explode right on the spot in a geyser of gore and vitriolic bile.

Longarm lazily shifted the muzzle of the big Lightning .44 back and forth, covering the wounded gunman's confused cohort and his boss. McCabe's bleeding guardian pawed at his thumbless hand, yelped, and hopped out the door onto Pecos's busy main thoroughfare.

Longarm returned McCabe's angry glare, smiled, and

said, "Guess he ain't as bad as you thought, McCabe. Otherwise, I'd be number twenty-six and ready for burying by now."

Constance Parker opened her mouth as wide as she could, wiggled a finger in each ear, and shook her head. Then she went back to staring her tormentor down like she just might reach over and slap him again, then snatch the beaklike nose right off his face.

As though the shooting had never taken place, Constance leaned back on her heels and snapped, "You don't know me well enough to call me a bitch, Mr. McCabe. Now I'll thank you to remove your mean-mouthed self and your thuggish employees from the property of my recently departed uncle. It would be to my personal liking, and preference, if you never darkened the door of this business again."

McCabe continued to glower at Longarm, who smiled in his most winning way and shrugged.

"Shoulda known you 'uz the one what blasted that bandit out by Turkey Rock," McCabe growled.

Longarm's sarcastic smile bled away. "How'd you know about that, McCabe?"

A wickedly evil grin creaked across McCabe's face. "News travels fast in a small town, mister. Valentine Devine's canoe-sized feet hadn't even touched the ground when he went to tellin' everyone in sight all about how a feller a-ridin' on his coach had dropped the hammer on a highwayman out by Turkey Rock earlier this mornin'. Even hinted as how you might be some kinda lawman. Probably still out there in the street a-yammerin' like an escapee from an insane asylum. Man couldn't keep a secret if'n he was foreman of an Austin grand jury."

"While I would have preferred that Mr. Devine kept today's events to himself for a spell, the fact that I'm *somewhat* known now is of no real consequence," said Longarm.

"It would've come to light sooner or later. All you really need to concern yourself with is that I'm here on special assignment to look into some unsolved mail thefts and a murder. Maybe even help your local constabulary with some stock-stealin' problems. You'd best make sure you've had no part in such shenanigans."

The flame-faced McCabe turned and stomped toward the store's open door, but appeared to think better of leaving and stopped. He whipped about and shook a knotted finger in Constance's face. Then he turned it on Longarm like it was an aimed dueling pistol and bellowed, "You two might as well know that what just transpired here ain't nowheres near the end of this dance. Just you wait and see, you son of a bitch. You, too, missy. You ain't heard the last of Fowler Mc-Cabe. Not by a long damned shot. Nobody treats me like a redheaded stepchild in my own town, or insults my integrity and gets away with it. When this whole dance all shakes out, I'll own this fuckin' place, and the both of you'll be on your way back to wherever you came from empty-handed. Just you wait and see, by God."

With that ominous pronouncement, the lanky scarecrow stumbled for the door, pushing his fat-gutted guardian ahead of him. Once they'd made it to the boardwalk, and Longarm had closed and locked the door behind them, he could still hear McCabe yelling, "What the hell are the pair of you good for? Worthless sons of bitches! Neither one of you's worth the powder to blow you to perdition!"

Longarm looked around from the door in time to spot Horace Westbrook fanning himself with his fancy black hat.

"God Almighty, folks. That was about as close as I ever want to get to dyin' an ugly, brutal death," Westbrook gushed.

"Oh, I don't think anyone of us was ever within shoutin' distance of dyin', Mr. Westbrook," Longarm said.

"I fear you're not as well acquainted with Fowler Mc-Cabe and his crew of killers as I am, sir. Many's the poor soul who has crossed that evil man and lived to regret it. Or, perhaps I should have said, not lived to regret it. Whole town's terrified of the man. And with good reason. Every word he spoke was the God's truth. He's a dangerous man. Very dangerous. Nefarious in every fiber of his being."

Constance brought the conversation back to practical matters when she said, "Can you recommend a decent place to spend the night, Mr. Westbrook?"

The lawyer brightened up. "Oh, that won't be necessary, Miss Parker. The entire upper floor of this building is four rooms of well-appointed and roomy living space. Two are bedrooms. Your uncle decorated the entire area with the absolute finest in furnishings shipped here from St. Louis. I think you'll find the space most accommodating."

"Well, then," Longarm said. "Seems everything has worked out just fine, Miss Constance. I'll just hustle on down to the Conklin Brothers depot, retrieve your bags, and have them brought to you forthwith."

"Most kind of you, Marshal Long."

Horace Westbrook looked puzzled. "Did you say, Marshal Long, Miss Parker?"

"Oh, my, Custis, appears I, too, have made a singular mistake and revealed your true identity."

Longarm dismissed the apology with the wave of a hand. "Well, I had hoped to move around town without creating any undue discomfort amongst the natives. Get the lay of the land, as it were. 'Course, if Valentine Devine's already gone and spilled the beans to everyone passin' in Pecos's main thoroughfare, this conversation doesn't mean a bloody thing."

Westbrook made a childlike motion as though padlocking his mouth. "Even if it isn't still necessary, my lips are sealed, Marshal Long. No one will hear of your true identity from me."

"Good enough. Why don't you look over your living quarters, Miss Constance, and I'll go see to your luggage. Pretty sure there's men a-hangin' 'round the depot who'll jump at the chance to make a dollar or two just for totin' your goods back this way. Have 'em all here for you quick as I can."

As the rangy lawman pulled the store's door open, Constance called out, "Do hurry back, Custis. Given what I just saw and heard, I don't feel at all comfortable with this situation in the least. That man gave me the worst case of creeping chicken flesh I've had in years. Last time I remember such fear and loathing was the first time I heard the tale of the wailing banshees of classic literature."

Longarm turned, tipped his hat, and smiled. "Don't worry, Miss Constance. You're entirely safe. Any banshees show up in Pecos, they'll have to deal with me." To his great satisfaction, he got the distinct impression that the beautiful Constance Parker blushed.

Chapter 11

Compared to most of the rough wayside inns Longarm usually picked as a place to stay while out on one of Billy Vail's assignments, the second-floor accommodations at the Orient Hotel of Pecos, Texas, bordered on the downright luxurious. Impressive, deep, colorful carpets decorated the floor. A fine, well-ticked mattress on the bed awaited any tired traveler. Unblemished mirrors hung on recently papered walls. There was a dresser, wardrobe, two chairs, and most important of all, a set of double windows that overlooked the town's hustling main thoroughfare.

Directly across the street below his convenient perch, and in full view when he loafed near the windows and fired up a cheroot, stood the impressive edifice of McCabe's Pecos Emporium. The deep, spacious, shaded veranda was littered with price-tagged, hand-tooled saddles, galvanized washtubs, hickory ax handles, several racks of ready-made clothing, and other such desirable merchandise. All was displayed in a manner guaranteed to get the tight-fisted traveler or local shopper inside.

Two doors down, and on the same side of the street, was

a likely-looking gambling and watering hole named the Palace Saloon. Several doors farther on from the drinking establishment's bright red batwings, Longarm could see the sign for Marshal Manny Frazier's office and city jail.

As far as Longarm was concerned, he'd stepped into about as much in the way of luxury and convenience as any man could want. Best of all, the whole shebang was within easy walking distance of Clegg's Mercantile and, of course, the astonishingly beautiful person of Miss Constance Parker.

As he puffed at a recently fired nickel cheroot, Longarm's concentrated attention was drawn to the busy entrance of McCabe's mercantile outfit. He pulled the window curtain and gauzy sheer back with one finger and watched as the black-garbed owner of the place and the blubbery henchman who looked like he'd eaten his own brother stepped from the store's doorway and into the orange-hued, afternoon sunlight.

McCabe used a talonlike finger and emphatically punched the beefy ruffian's shoulder. Hard. The fat man, whose pants looked like they could have been split up the side and made into a tent for an entire family of traveling gypsies, nodded as though his worthless life depended on it.

The heated conversation lasted but a few seconds. Then the fat man huffed, puffed, and waddled his way to a nearby hitch rail and laboriously climbed aboard a monstrous chestnut hay burner that could easily have been related, in some twisted, grotesque way, to a circus elephant. He urged the poor overburdened beast east on Main Street, but the horse, to Longarm's grinning delight, appeared content to take its time getting wherever the intended object of the ride happened to be—no matter how hard the fat man kicked at the poor beast's bulky sides. Given the events that had transpired earlier that very afternoon, Longarm thought the whole scene just a bit curious, and wondered what the despicable McCabe and his tub-of-guts bullyboy might be up to.

Longarm locked his room, then headed for the hotel lobby. He eased onto the boardwalk, made certain no threat appeared imminent, then strolled across the busy street and started for Manny Frazier's office. He'd gone but a few steps when Valentine Devine cruised up, hands in his pockets and looking sheepish. Devine reminded Longarm of an oversized kid that'd just got caught out behind the barn with an enormous paw stuck in his little sister's drawers.

"Done just like you said, Marshal Long. Got some Messicans to carry all a Miss Parker's bags over to Clegg's. Made sure the whole kit and kaboodle got put exactly where she wanted 'em fore I left, too. Fine woman, that 'un. Goodlookin', too. Them Messicans wuz right pleased with the silver dollar I give each one of 'em. Buy a pile a tacos with a silver dollar."

Longarm kept walking. He nodded, then said, "Well, that's fine, Val. Sounds like everything worked out just fine. Trust you found Miss Parker in good health?"

Devine scratched his meaty, stubble-covered chin, then his neck. "Yeah. Guess you could say that. Looked okay to me. Far as I could tell anyway. But you know, Marshal Long, if'n I 'uz that little gal, I'd be damned careful. Whoever went and kilt Mr. Clegg didn't do it jus' fer the fun a the thang. No, sirree bob, sir. They 'uz after somethin' for certain sure, and I 'uz a-thinkin' as how maybe they didn't git it yet."

"Well, you're probably right about that, Val. But I don't believe she has anything to worry about at the moment."

Devine nodded. "Ah. If'n you say so. Just that dead folks always get me to a-thinkin' and a-worryin'. Cain't help myself, you know. Where you headed, Marshal?"

"Local lawman's office yonder. Figured since everyone in town probably already knows who I am, might as well pay him a visit and get all the necessary palaverin' out of the way."

Devine jammed his hands back in his pockets. "Well, now, you know, Marshal Long, I'm real sorry 'bout lettin' that particular cat outta the bag. My fault altogether and I'm terrible sorry 'bout the whole thang."

"Truly?"

"Yessir, I surely am. But, hell, I just couldn't help myself. Bein' as how we'd had so much previous trouble out on the road from Toya an' all, havin' you up top and a-blastin' that holdup artist the way you did, why, it wuz just by God poetic, that's what it wuz. And I just got to figurin' as how folks needed to know all 'bout the thang."

"But I asked you not to tell anyone about me."

"Yep. Yep, you surely did at that. But truth is, an' I prolly shoulda tole you before, everyone what knows me is fully aware that, for me, keepin' a secret is harder'n keepin' a wildcat under a number-three washtub."

"Fine time to tell me."

"I know. But, hell, I've had folks as have said I should jus' go on ahead an' keep a sock in my mouth jus' so's my foot'll be warm when I go an' stick 'er in there." Devine let out a nervous-sounding snicker at his own joke, and then cuffed Longarm on the shoulder like they were long-lost brothers sharing old family secrets.

In spite of himself, Longarm grinned. "Well, no need to worry yourself any, Val. Figure there's no real harm done. Couple a piddly-assed mail robberies and some stock theft don't really require all that much in the way of real secretive, federal lawman-type skulkin' around anyway. 'Course the murder of your friend Harley Beckwith is a bit more problematic in a legal-technicality kind of a way. I personally feel the Pecos city marshal, Manny Frazier, and his crew of deputies should be responsible for that one. Truth is, I still haven't figured out why my boss bothered to send me all the way out here on this chicken-wrangling expedition."

Devine chuckled at the chicken-wrangler joke, cuffed Longarm on the shoulder again, and to the lawman's amazement somehow managed to vanish just about the time they arrived at Marshal Manny Frazier's office door. One second he was right at Longarm's elbow, and the next second he was gone.

Longarm cast a curious glance up and down the street, but Devine appeared to have simply evaporated like a monstrous gob of spit on a hot stove lid. Longarm shook his head in wonderment and reached for the knob to the city marshal's office. Unsuspecting fingers had barely touched the piece of polished brass when a hailstorm of bullets peppered the door frame all around him. Wood splinters filled the air like elongated raindrops.

Instinctive, lifesaving reflexes took over and instantly forced Longarm through the doorway and onto the floor of the office in a flopping heap. He rolled to safety beneath the office's front window just barely ahead of a second volley of blazing-hot lead that peppered the floor inside the doorway and turned the sheet of beveled plate glass overhead into a sparkling cloud of buzzing, jagged bees.

His back decorated with busted chunks of wood from the bullet-riddled door frame and shards of splintered glass, Longarm crawfished to the nearest corner. He sat up, snatched the Colt from its holster, then scrunched himself into a defensive knot. He slanted a quick glance toward the back of the office, and spotted Marshal Manny Frazier lying on his stomach behind a battered banker's desk.

At first Longarm thought Pecos's primary lawman might have been blasted into something akin to a flour sifter by the blistering fusillade of bullets and was already shaking hands with St. Peter at the Pearly Gates. To his shock and surprise, the dapper little man, who bore a striking resemblance to a Fort Worth gambler friend of Longarm's named Luke Short, moved, cast a baleful stare toward the corner, and said, "Good to see you again, Custis. Leastways, I think it's good to see you."

As abruptly as the blasting started, it stopped. Longarm shot a quick, searching glance over the office's windowsill. No one was in sight. The street appeared completely deserted. He brought his pistol up at darting shadows on the rooftop of a saloon named the Gem directly across the street, but couldn't get anything like a good target.

Frazier stumbled to his feet and set to brushing himself off. He ran fingers through a thick head of black pomaded hair, then twisted his droopy mustache. "Tell you the truth, Custis, I'm about to get damned tired of this kinda shit."

Longarm stood, but remained pressed into the corner, pistol at the ready. "Whaddaya mean, tired of this kinda shit, Manny? Somebody take a shot at you more'n once?"

Pecos's town marshal righted his overturned chair and flopped into it like a man whose mainspring had just about wound completely down. "Been a-happenin' about once every other month or so for nigh on a year. Ever since me and Bud Miller started pokin' around and tryin' to put an end to some of the stock theft around this fuckin' burg."

Concerned that ambushing bastards might still be lurking

about, Longarm kept his back to the wall as he edged his way around the office. Eventually, he found a comfortable spot beside Frazier's well-stocked gun rack. From the new vantage point he could watch the door and, at the same time, see through the now-missing window to the street outside.

"Sounds like you just might have a pretty good idea who's doin' the stealin', or at least some of the thieves think you do."

Frazier shoved a chair toward Longarm with his foot. "Might as well have a seat."

"Seem right unconcerned about this whole mess, Manny," Longarm said as he pulled the chair to his sheltered spot by the gun rack and nestled into it.

"Aw, hell, nothin' to worry about now, Custis. Them ole boys are surely gone till the next go-round. They don't usually shoot but a time or two, then skedaddle. Just tryin' to put the fear of God into me most likely. Have to get away 'fore somebody spots 'em. 'Sides, near as I can tell, the stupid sons a bitches cain't shoot for spit."

Longarm nodded. "Well, you might have something there. Sure missed the hell outta me, and I couldn't a made a better target lest I stood in the street with a bull's-eye painted on my back and chest."

Frazier grinned and shook his head. "Irritatin' shit is gettin' right tiresome, though. Ya know, think I'm gonna board my winder up this time around 'stead a replacin' it. Or maybe get some heavy-duty shutters put up. Somethin' like four-by-four boards held up with iron brackets. Damned glass is gettin' expensive. And, yes, I for damned sure know who's responsible for all the rustlin', thievin', and shootin' goin' on 'round these parts. Hell, you name the crime, he's most likely behind it."

"Wouldn't be a walkin' corpse name of Fowler McCabe, would it?"

"Ah, you've done gone and throwed your saddle on the right horse now, Deputy U.S. Marshal Long. Bet the two a you've already met. Done got closer'n kissin' cousins, I vow," Frazier said, and let a rueful grin etch its way across his handsome face.

"Well, I wouldn't say we're at that point in our relationship where if I have a biscuit, ole Fowler's gonna git half 'cause I love him so much, but we have met and said howdy."

Pecos's harried city marshal snatched a drawer of his desk open and pulled out a bottle of gold-label Maryland rye and a pair of almost clean glasses. He filled both tumblers. Shoved one across the desk to Longarm, then leaned back in his chair and took a sip from the other.

"My favorite brand. I'm by God touched, Manny," Longarm muttered.

"Damnation, it's sure 'nuff good stuff, Custis. Been drinkin' your choice a panther piss ever since you introduced me to it, back when we run Gopher Riley to ground for killin' that judge over in San Angelo. 'Member that 'un? Musta been ten years ago."

Custis Long took a slug from his drink, then said, "I remember. Lotta water under the bridge since them days."

"Yep. Lotta years."

"Tell me, Manny, if you know McCabe's responsible for the intemperate acts of stock theft, attempted murder, destruction of city property, shootin' the hell outta your office, and such, why haven't you thrown his sorry ass in a cell yet, or killed him?"

"Number-one reason right at the top of the old lawman's handy-dandy list of excuses for not doing what he knows is right—can't catch the evil bastard at any of it. He's one sneaky-smart son of a bitch, Custis. Don't even carry a gun. Hires men to do his shootin'."

Frazier leaned his complaining banker's chair back as far as it would go, then propped both booted feet on his desk. He sat with the drink resting on his belly, like he might just go to sleep. "Besides, figure if Ole Fowler *really* wanted me dead, I wouldn't have any more pulse than a busted pitchfork right now. 'Course he'd best hurry, 'cause I might not be here too much longer. Gettin' tired of bein' shot at."

"Given the fact that less than two hours ago I blew the thumb off'n one a McCabe's bullyboys, figured for sure all the shootin' was directed at *me*."

Frazier threw his head back and laughed. "Do tell. Hadn't heard about that dustup. Usually, if anything don't go Fowler's way, he's right here in front of my desk gripin' and a-grousin', bitchin' and moanin'. Man complains more'n a kicked dog. Seems to be one of those folks who firmly believes that the squeakin' gate gets oiled. And Good God, he can squeak with the best of 'em."

"You think McCabe has a finger in the stock-thievin' pie that Billy Vail mentioned has you tied in knots?"

"Finger, hell. Son of a bitch has a whole hand in that 'un. Way I've got it figured, the scheme works like this. McCabe sits in the office of his mercantile store, in plain view of God and everybody in town. Crew a his cutthroats go out and steal every animal they can run off a some poor, pissant rancher's paltry piece a property out in the middle of Nowhere, Tejas. Within a week, all a them animals is in Mexico. 'Fore the poor rancher knows what hit him, the bank shows up with a foreclosure notice for nonpayment of this or that, and McCabe steps in and buys up the debt. He forces the rancher off the property and, lo and behold, Fowler McCabe, by virtue of the poor rancher's piss-poor luck, has miraculously become the biggest landowner west of Fort Worth."

Longarm threw down the rest of his drink, then muttered, "Sweet Jesus."

"Yeah, I've recently called on the Deity for heavenly help a number of times myself. Had my hands full ever since I took the job of town marshal. McCabe's like a Biblical Egyptian plague, and life as a lawman in Pecos's been a miserable mess. That's why I couldn't offer much in the way of help to Billy Vail in any investigation of them piddling mail robberies and Harley Beckwith's unfortunate murder. Be willin' to bet some a McCabe's bunch are behind both of 'em, but I've been busier'n a chicken drinkin' water out of a pie tin with other problems."

"McCabe got anybody of real quality workin' for him? Pair I met earlier today didn't show me much."

"Oh, of the near twenty I know about for certain that are on his payroll, he's got a couple a genuine, dyed-in-the-wool death dealers lurkin' around in the shadows. Kept a pretty tight rein on 'em up till now, though. Usually lets his run-a-the-mill thugs do most of the dirty work. Not sure which two you saw, but he's got as many as twenty a-workin' for him, in addition to all the folks he employs around town in one way or another."

"You know the names of these *genuine death dealers*?"

"Millard Tubbs for one."

"Damn."

"Yeah. But that ain't the half of it. Dorsey Barber for another."

"God Almighty, Manny. Don't know either of 'em, but I've heard enough about both of 'em. Get those two together and it's a wonder you don't have bodies piled up eyeball-deep right outside your office."

"Tell me 'bout it. But I ain't finished. There's rumors goin' 'round as how McCabe keeps Orpheus Stonehouse outta sight on his ranch a bit northwest of town—place named the Bar M. 'S where most a his bunch spends their time anyway. Rarely see any of 'em in town less McCabe has *business* to conduct with some a the local hoople-heads. Suppose he has Stonehouse around just in case he needs a proven butcher, you know."

"What about Tubbs and Barber?"

"They tend to hang 'round a couple a doors down the boardwalk at the Palace Saloon most times. Personally, I ain't never seen hide nor hair of Stonehouse. Could be he's nothin' more'n a heavy-duty windy whizzer McCabe's spreadin' just to scare folks. Then again, that don't mean the murderous bastard ain't skulkin' 'round somewheres just a-waitin' to pop up and kill the hell outta me, or anyone else as gets in McCabe's way."

Longarm hopped out of his chair. He waded through the wreckage of Frazier's shattered window and front door, stood next to the wall, and stared out at the street. Broken glass crunched beneath his feet. As though to himself, he said, "Know what I think, Manny? I think you might need a whole new approach to all your problems. Possible presence of Orpheus Stonehouse sure as hell puts a whole new wrinkle on the situation. Just adds to my feeling that McCabe's the kind of man a soft-glove approach just never works on. Yep, a whole new approach."

"New approach? What the hell does that mean?"

"Got any deputies?"

"Had three up till a week or so ago. They all quit. Worst was when they heard them tales about Stonehouse. Two of 'em walked off that same day."

"McCabe and men like those you just mentioned ain't gonna be easy to deal with. Only thing they understand is hot lead and the possibility of imminent death. Put killers like Tubbs, Barber, and Stonehouse under the control of a skunk of McCabe's caliber and you've got a problem that can only be solved one way."

"How's that?"

"Gonna have to get tougher'n a roll of brand-new barbed wire. Make life so uncertain for McCabe and his bunch, they either bet the whole stack, fold, or die."

"Mighty tough talk for a federal man, Custis. Just how far are you prepared to go?"

Longarm jerked the wobbly plank entry panel open. "Far as it takes. But I'd sure 'nuff feel a lot more comfortable if we had some help."

"Sorry. Life's tougher'n a wild pig's snout for a lawman in Pecos these days, Custis. Where you headed now?"

Pausing in the doorway, Longarm glanced into the street again. As he slipped out the Colt and checked its loads, he noticed small knots of inquisitive people gathered on the boardwalks and standing in the thoroughfare. Some pointed at the office's bullet-blasted facade and shook their heads. Others spoke to one another in hushed tones behind their hands.

Longarm reholstered the pistol, then said, "Think I'll stroll down the boardwalk to the Palace. Maybe play a little poker. Always has been my favorite way to get information. See if I can't stir the pot some."

"Best be careful, Custis. McCabe's boys are a nervous lot. 'Bout as nervous as a bunch a pigs in a packin'house. Ain't happened out in the open yet, but I'd bet they're not the least bit averse to gunnin' anyone as gets in their way. They've done as much before, if reputation means anything. Gettin' anyone to testify against 'em 'pears like it'd be a real trick to me. They could kill your or me and no one in Pecos would admit to seeing or hearing a thing."

Over his shoulder, Longarm said, "Tell you the God's truth, Manny. I'm countin' on that exact attitude. Can bet the ranch I'm countin' on it."

Chapter 12

A fingernail-shaped sliver of western sun cast lengthening shadows in a reddish smudge along Pecos's reviving central thoroughfare as Longarm eased up to the Palace Saloon's bloodred batwings. He placed one hand on the fancy, scrolled woodwork that decorated the door's upper edge, and gazed inside. The heavy odors of fresh sawdust on the floor, burning tobacco, liquor in all its various forms, and sweaty men wafted out through the open portal and assaulted his flared nostrils.

Casually, he lit a nickel cheroot and puffed it to life, then, for several seconds, intently peered inside again. His concentrated gaze moved from table to table in search of anything amiss. The pause gave his eyes plenty of time to adjust to the darker interior of the West Texas town's premier liquor-slinging and gambling establishment. Lighted coal-oil lanterns bathed the saloon's interior in a muted golden glow. When finally assured he wouldn't enter the cow-country cantina sun-blinded, he pushed through the swinging gates and quickly moved to the near end of an elaborate, opulently carved mahogany bar.

The enormous bar ran almost the entire length of the

oblong room from one end to the other—near thirty feet in all. It sported a gleaming, highly polished marble top, along with a varied, colorful, and well-stocked back bar. The brass foot rail beneath his boot glowed like burnished gold. Polished spittoons appeared to grow up next to the fancy footrest every two or three feet like shiny cabbages.

Instead of the usual oil painting that always depicted a well-endowed, naked, reclining woman, or massive beveled mirror, the wall of the Palace Saloon's back bar sported the mounted head of an enormous deer with a rack of horns that surpassed any Longarm had ever seen. This manly, fur-covered decoration set the tone for the rest of the well-appointed watering hole.

Nearly every bare spot of wall space in the entire joint sported the head of a fearsome, tusk-jawed javelina, prong-horned antelope, elk, long-horned steer, raccoon, beaver, wildcat, cougar, or bear.

On a raised platform at the far end of the room, a slick-pated piano player, wearing a bookkeeper's visor, fancy silk vest, and bright red cravat, puffed a cigar the size of an ax handle. Stubby fingers danced across yellowed ivories as he pounded out an off-key, metallic, tinkling tune.

A hunchbacked bartender, wearing fancy garters on both arms, who looked every minute of a hundred years old, spotted Longarm and hobbled over like a crippled squirrel. He wiped at a spot on the already glistening bar, then offered up a crack-lipped, snaggle-toothed smile.

"What can I do you fer today, mister?"

Longarm glanced past the bartender and checked the players, drinkers, and idlers at each table again before he relaxed, and leaned over the bar on one elbow. "Place looks like a museum for lost animal heads, pardner."

The bald, mustachioed bartender let out a chuckling snort, then scratched his wrinkled, leathery neck with a liver-spotted hand. "Yeah. Well, feller what opened this joint some years back fancied hisself quite the hunter. Appears to have kilt one of just about everything a man can shoot and skin. Got married six times, too, as I recall. Wonder they ain't two or three of his former wives up there with all them bears, beavers, and wildcats."

"Ah, well, all that goes a long way toward explaining the choice of furnishings. Take it from what you just said, the great hunter no longer owns this place."

"Naw. He went and got his silly self rudely kilt several years ago. Went out on one a them hunts he favored so much. Tryin' to murder the hell outta some kinda furry critter or t'other. Musta been a-lookin' in the wrong direction. Stepped on a big ole rattler 'bout the size of a barmaid's leg. Monster snapper jumped up an' got 'im right in the crotch. Way I heard it, his entire business swelled up like somethin' rotten. Died deader'n a busted hoe handle in less'n a hour."

"Helluva terrible way to go out."

"Bad 'un, all right. Friends that 'uz with 'im kilt the snake. That's the skin a-hangin' on the wall over the pianner player's head."

Longarm glanced at the reptile's hide and shook his head. "Jesus. Saw the thing. Thought it was a bed blanket made to look like a snake's skin. Christ Almighty, big sucker musta been ten feet long."

"Twelve. You know, I've always figured the feller what got bit probably called on the Lord, like you just done. When the snake got 'im, that is. Wasn't there to witness the bite an' all, but I'll bet he went to hollerin' for Jesus sure as Hell's hot."

Longarm shook his head once more, then said, "Saw a sign in your front window that claims the Palace Saloon has honest-to-God *cold* beer, ole-timer."

113

"That we do, sir. Coldest east of El Paso or west of Fort Worth. Have our very own, modern, up-to-the-minute ice-making facility right here in Pecos. Been in operation near a year."

Longarm tossed a coin onto the bar. "Well, bring me one of them bad boys. Coldest you've got."

Bartender hobbled back to a spot midway of the bar, drew the beer, then, with obvious pride, waddled over and set the frosty glass in front of his newest customer. "Messican brew. Dark, rich, almost like syrup. Mighty good stuff. One thing 'bout Messicans, they sure's hell know how to brew great beer."

Longarm raised the glass, nodded, then took a long, satisfying gulp. Wiped the foam off his mustache, smacked his lips several times, and then shook his head. "Damn, as you said, that is some mighty good stuff. Uh-h-h, what's your name, friend?"

Proud drink slinger beamed with delight and went to wiping the bar again. "Mike Pincus, sir. And yours?"

"Long. Custis Long. Pleased to make your acquaintance, Mike." Longarm made another quick survey around the room, then leaned over the bar and motioned Pincus closer. He pulled his wallet out, displayed the twinkling deputy U.S. marshal's badge inside, then as quickly slipped it back into his jacket pocket. In a near-whisper, he said, "Wonder if you could tell me something, Mike."

Pincus wiped at a spot near Longarm's frosty glass, then glanced over his shoulder as though to make sure no one was listening in. "Well, if'n we can make it appear to all the tipplers in attendance that we're just passin' the time of day, I will if'n I can, Marshal."

"Do you know if either Millard Tubbs or Dorsey Barber are sittin' in on any of the games today?"

Pincus's eyes did a sneaky dart sidewise. Then he jerked

his head in the general direction of a table at the back of the room near the piano stand. "Tubbs. That's him back yonder. Big ole boy a-wearin' the wide-brimmed, palm-leaf sombrero. Couple a little tin bells attached to the back of the hat. Hear him a-tinklin' all the way up here. Wouldn't go a-messin' with him if'n I wuz you, Marshal. He's a bad 'un. Be willin' to bet money that if'n you posted a letter addressed to the Devil, it'd get delivered to that skunk."

"What about Barber?"

"Ain't seen him today, thank God. And Lord help us, he's a bad 'un, too. Maybe worse'n Tubbs, if that's even possible. Pair of 'em wuz born with reserved seats in Hell from the minute they popped outta their mamas' bellies. Figure they'll be a-sittin' on Satan's right hand the very second someone manages to send 'em that well-deserved direction."

"Met a feller name of Orpheus Stonehouse yet, Mike?"

"Nope. Not yet. Ain't lookin' forward to the event either. I've heard stories 'bout 'im. From what folks say, Stonehouse's worse than these other two put together—a real fire eater with a well-earned reputation for general, run-of-the-mill cussidness. Heard tell as how he kills people just to watch 'em bleed out."

Longarm went thoughtful for several seconds. He sipped at his beer, then said, "Fellers playin' poker with Tubbs mind havin' strange money on the table?"

Pincus grinned. "Oh, hell, no. They don't care one way or the other. But do be careful of Tubbs. Man cain't play for shit, but hates to lose."

"I know the type."

"Most times, them other boys let him win just enough to keep him happy. 'Specially when he's been drinkin' pretty heavy. On top a everything else, he's a mean drunk." Pincus cupped a hand over his mouth. "He's done shot several fellers what beat him at the pasteboards, or pissed him off over nothin' in particular. Shot them poker players, then picked up all the money on the table and walked out like he owned the place."

"Marshal Frazier didn't do anything about the shootings?"

"Not much he could do. Every time ole Tubbs was involved in a shootin', witnesses or other boys at the table proved so scared, they all swore them poor dead fellers drew down on Tubbs first. And a 'course he just naturally had to defend himself, don't you know."

Longarm took his glass and started toward the far end of the bar. "Thanks, Mike. Keep an eye peeled my direction. Love this cold beer. You can keep 'em comin' till I tell you to stop."

"Be lookin' out for you, Marshal. Send one a the girls with a fresh glass anytime you get low. Just you give me the high sign. She'll be right over."

Longarm absentmindedly acknowledged the bartender with his free hand. He edged past several laughing females, who hopped from one group of men to the next—gatherings of happy, run-of-the-mill drunks, tables of gregarious gamblers. Then Longarm stopped near the piano player.

He leaned against the back wall, studied Tubbs and the men he played poker with, and sipped at his beer. After several minutes of calculated scrutiny, he strolled over to the table of cardplayers and grasped the back of an empty chair.

"You gents mind if I sit in with you?"

The heads of the other men at the table all turned toward Tubbs at the same time, as though seeking his approval before offering the stranger an invitation to sit. The gunman slowly raised his dead-eyed gaze and eyeballed Longarm as though he'd just found an enormous gob of fresh horseshit on the sole of his boot.

Tubbs pulled a gooey, well-chewed cheroot from the corner of a twisted, snarling mouth, then growled, "Ain't never seen you 'round here afore, have I, mister?"

Longarm flashed a toothy, appealing grin. "True enough. Just passin' through, friend. On my way to Barstow. Big horse ranch over that way. Kermit Wickett's Triple W. Buyin' remounts for the cavalry down at Fort Davis."

Longarm knew the hoax contained just enough truth to fool, or at least confuse, anyone not native to the area. It also planted the seed in Tubbs's mind that Longarm was a man with plenty of cash in his pocket.

In a telling display of grandiose pomposity, Tubbs regally motioned toward the empty chair and said, "Well, go right on ahead and take a seat. Always glad to have new money in the game."

The other players smiled, nodded their approval, and beckoned him to sit. The man on Longarm's immediate left was a rail-thin professional gambler dressed in a stovepipe hat, well-worn plaid suit, and frayed-at-the-collar shirt. He grinned as he said, "Yes, friend, please do take a seat. Perhaps some new blood can change my luck, by God. Way the pasteboards 've been runnin', might have to give up poker and take a job preachin' in one of the local churches."

A rangy, sunbaked brush popper across the table perked up and added, "Ain't that the truth. Hell, I might as well follow the call as well and be one of your plate-passin' deacons. Seems like Ole Tubbs is the only one at this table what can win a cent today." His open, friendly grin bled away when Tubbs shot a slit-eyed glance in the wrangler's direction.

The third man at the table, other than Tubbs, also appeared to be a professional. His luck or skill evidently exceeded that of his more poorly attired, unlucky counterpart. He was dressed in a smart, spotless black frock coat with fancy wine-colored, gold-trimmed silk vest, blindingly white shirt, and bloodred cravat with diamond stickpin. Clean-shaven, with straight hair pomaded and slicked back, the man appeared fully capable of taking every last cent on the table with about as much ease as the farmer who went fishing with a box of dynamite.

The gambler cast a less-than-uninterested glance at Longarm. He snatched up a tumbler of whiskey, took a sip that barely dampened his tongue, then nodded as though bored near to tears.

Longarm pulled a rickety, straight-backed, cane-bottomed chair away from the table. On the sly, as he bent over to take his wobbly seat, the wary lawman slipped his Colt from its oiled holster and laid it in his lap. He doubted that an overly lubricated Millard Tubbs, who smelled like he'd just crawled out of a wolf's den saturated in hundred-fifty-proof rye, was any match for him in a straight-up pistol fight. But he also figured that the added edge of having the gun ready could easily mean the razor's edge of difference between surviving a blistering gun battle and the rather bothersome alternative.

Unable to control it, he let a barely perceptible grin play across his lips. He felt as though he'd succeeded in laying the trap, and given the kind of man he figured Tubbs to be, all he had to do now was throw out the right bait and wait for the predictable reaction.

Chapter 13

It took less than half an hour for Longarm to realize that the besotted Millard Tubbs played poker like a stroke-addled, old-maid schoolteacher. The brooding gunman's tells were so obvious as to border on the amusing. The insolent, drunken bully bet heavily when holding anything more weighty than an ace, whether his piss-poor hand had any chance of winning or not. A lowly pair of deuces, and the man bet like he had the best hand and all the money in the world.

Perhaps most revealing of his lack of skill was that Tubbs always folded when little or nothing came his way, and he had a glaring habit of rubbing his nose just before he pitched in his hand. During those times when he dropped out of play, the churlish lout drank and berated the other men at the table to "hurry the hell up so's I can get back in and win back the money I jist had to ante up."

In spite of Tubbs's obvious lack of talent for the game, the other players, especially the two professionals, deferred to the ornery skunk in every possible instance. Just as the bartender Mike Pincus had warned, the trio appeared to conspire at seeing to it that the sullen snake won just enough to keep his rude demeanor from getting any worse, or being aimed in their general direction.

A bit more than an hour into the uncomfortable festivities, a fresh beer appeared on the table at Longarm's elbow. He glanced up from his cards and gazed into the gloriously beautiful face of a pouty-mouthed, dark-skinned Mexican girl who said, "Mr. Mike had to leave. Said he'd return in half an hour or so. He told me to take very good care of you, Señor. *Es mi gusto.*"

She was barely five feet tall, full-lipped, and lusciously bare-shouldered, and the raven-haired, brown-eyed gal's ample breasts brushed against Longarm's upper arm. The rustic beauty's rough, cotton blouse was cut so low, it strained mightily to cover dark, silver-dollar-sized areolas tipped with stiff nipples as big as a man's thumb.

To Longarm's pleasure and surprise, the girl moved behind him and leaned so close, he could feel the pressure of her enormous breasts against his neck. She gently placed her hands on his shoulders and seductively swayed from side to side, using her melon-sized rack in an abbreviated but glaringly obvious dance of seduction.

All of a sudden, her hot, wet breath tickled his ear. In a purring voice only he could hear, she whispered, "Should you require *anything,* and I do mean *anything at all,* Señor, wave, or simply call out for Conchita. Conchita is always ready, Señor."

Tubbs, who'd been steadily losing to Longarm ever since he let the man sit down, glanced up from his cards, went red in the face, and snorted, "Get the fuck away from him, you silly fuckin' bitch. Man's got nigh on two hundred dollars of my money, and I don't want any a you flat backers a-takin' his attention off'n the game. Traipse your worthless ass on back to where you came from."

Smiling as though he'd not even spoken, Conchita

twitched her way over to Tubbs's side. Tight, muscular hips rolled under her colorful peasant dress like puppies under a blanket. She placed a hand on the angry tough's arm and, while continuing to flirtatiously stare Longarm directly in the eye, crooned, "No need to be angry, Señor. Conchita is only carrying out the instructions of *mi jefe*. Conchita always does as her *jefe* says. *Always*."

Like a striking diamondback, Tubbs's arm shot forward with a speed that belied his ceaseless, soused elbow-bending. He grabbed the girl by the wrist and gave it a vicious twist.

Conchita cried out in obvious pain and went to her knees. "Please, Señor. Conchita meant no harm. Please do not hurt me."

Squeezed from the corner of the girl's eye, Longarm spotted a huge, crystalline tear that rolled down her face and hung on her jaw. He stacked his hand and dropped it on the table behind a jumbled pile of multicolored chips. He then slipped a hand into his lap and wrapped eager fingers around the cut-bone grips of his double-action blaster. Tubbs had finally gone too far.

The other gamblers at the table barely heard him when Longarm growled, "Let 'er go, you stupid son of a bitch."

The bells dangling from the back of Tubbs's sweat-stained palm-leaf hat jingled when he jerked his head around to glare across the table. Squint-eyed, nearly purple-faced, and gritting his teeth, he held the girl in a viselike grip, and didn't appear prone to comply with Longarm's threatening demand.

Stringy slobbers ran down his stubble-covered chin when he snarled, "Well, now, you can shut the fuck up, mister. Might just get up from here and kick yer stupid ass till yer nose bleeds. I'll let this little hot tamale go when I goddamn well please, you horse-buyin', card-bendin' weasel. Fuck with me and I'll squash the both of ya like a couple a shit-rollin' dung beetles."

Tubbs had unwittingly provided exactly the opportunity Longarm had planned on and patiently waited for. "Did you just call me a cheat, Tubbs? Sure 'nuff sounded that way. *Card bender* I think was the phrase you used. As in, bendin' cards in an effort to bilk other players out of their money. Seems like you're sayin' I'm the kinda feller's on a first-name basis with the bottom of the deck."

Tubbs glared at Longarm and twisted the girl's arm again—more cruelly than before. Conchita's agony became more pronounced. Tears flowed freely, but she appeared reluctant to cry out again.

"I'll do as I please with this pepper-bellied cunt. And I'll call you anything I want, you mealy-mouthed cocksucker. Never seen you afore today. Come waltzin' in here, flop your sorry ass down at my table. Take my money jus' like you own the damned place. Really pisses me off, you know?"

Longarm grinned. "Reason you're losin' is because you're about half as smart as a snubbin' post, and you can't play poker worth a tinker's damn. From what I hear, near everybody in town, and their distant cousins in Austin, knows exactly how bad a poker player you really are."

Tubbs grunted like he'd been slapped with an open palm.

Longarm shoved the gunman over the edge when he said, "Hell, I'd bet to teach an ignorant jackass like you something as simple as pullin' on your own boots would prove about as difficult as playin' a harp with a claw hammer."

Tubbs pushed Conchita aside, then roared to his feet as the teary-eyed girl scuttled to safety on her hands and knees. The drunken gunman towered over the table and shook a finger in Longarm's face. "I've killed a dozen men for less'n what you just said, you fancy-talkin' bastard."

Out of sight, Longarm brought his pistol around. He

aimed up through the felt-covered poker table at a spot he estimated was just above Tubbs's fancy silver belt buckle. Way he had it figured, even if the shot didn't kill the stupid son of a bitch, it would put his arrogant ass on the floor in a painful doubled-up knot sure as getting hit in the gut with a flaming sledgehammer.

In an effort to appear the part of magnanimous peacemaker, Longarm said, "Why don't you sit back down, stop drinkin', and start payin' attention? Even somebody as stupid as you are might learn something from these gentlemen we're playin' with. Any one of 'em could take every cent you ever had and you'd never know how it happened—if they weren't afraid you'd go and start actin' like an idiot."

A pulsating vein in Tubbs's temple grew to the size of a grown man's index finger and appeared on the verge of bursting. "Stand up, you slick-talkin' son of a bitch. Gonna put enough holes in your hide so's you'll look like my grandma's flour sifter when I'm finished blastin' the shit outta you." He jerked his coattail back to reveal a Remington Model 1875 single-action Army pistol strapped high on his hip.

The other three gamblers dipped their heads, then scooted away from the table, scattered, and hastily headed for the nearest exit or sheltered spot of perceived safety. Almost everyone else within earshot of the angry disagreement followed suit. A sizable contingent of the morbidly curious stayed on the scene, peeked over the Palace's long, marble-topped bar, and anxiously waited for blood to be spilled.

Longarm said, "Wouldn't do anything ill-advised, Tubbs. You make the mistake of being the third man to pull a gun on me today and I'll send you to Jesus on an outhouse door."

Tubbs appeared on the verge of apoplexy when he

grunted, "Mighty fuckin' confident of yourself there, ain't you, mister?"

Longarm stared back into the burly gunfighter's lifeless eyes. "Confidence has got nothin' to do with it, Tubbs. You're overmatched, and way too witless to know it."

"How you figure that 'un?"

"Under this table there's a Colt Lightning pistol aimed at your guts. Make the wrong move and you're gonna force me to punch your ticket to the hereafter."

"You're a-bluffin'. Just like all them poker pots you scraped up. Ain't got no more shit in your hand now than you had then."

"Don't push your luck, you dumb bastard."

Tubbs yelped, "Well, by God, that rips the rag off the bush." He went for the Remington on his hip, but his fingers had barely touched the grips when Longarm touched off a deafening blast that erupted through the tabletop in a shower of wood chunks, flying poker chips, and fluttering cards. The concussion from the blast blew out several coal-oil lamps hanging from hammered-iron sconces on the wall nearby.

White-hot lead carrying a fist-sized wad of wood splinters hit Millard Tubbs just below the breastbone. Table fragments peppered the man's chest as the .44-caliber slug sliced through his body like a well-sharpened butcher's knife. The heavy bullet gathered up part of his heart, pushed the whole mess through a rib in his back, and painted the wall behind him with a geyser of blood, bone, and gore.

Longarm brought the pistol from beneath the table and zeroed in on the gunman's head. He watched in awe as Tubbs swayed like a weeping willow on a South Texas creek bank and grabbed at the bubbling, frothy hole in his chest. The long-barreled Remington slipped from uncooperative fingers, ricocheted off the poker table, and landed on the floor at his unsteady feet with a resounding, dust-raising thump. Then he clawed his splinter-riddled vest open and ripped at the shirt beneath.

Foamy, bright red blood gurgled from the nickel-sized opening in Tubbs's body. He stared down at the hole and shook his head, then cast an odd, unbelieving look back at Longarm, who calmly watched the man's life drain away.

"Damnation. You shot me, you sneaky son of a bitch," Tubbs gasped, then flopped back into his chair. Blood pooled in the chair's seat and dripped onto the floor. Barely able to hold his head up, he groaned, then said, "Ain't nobody ever been able to shoot me in a fair fight afore."

Longarm grinned across the table at the dying gunman. "Wasn't exactly a fair fight, Tubbs. You're right. I am a sneaky son of a bitch. Must admit, I fudged just a bit. But not at the cards. You lost fair and square there. Mainly 'cause everything I said to you was true. Shoulda left the girl alone. Just cannot abide rude behavior, especially when it comes to women. Really shortsighted of you to act that way around a gentleman. Honest to God, if brains were gunpowder, Tubbs, you wouldn't have enough to blow the ass off a gnat."

Tubbs's hands dropped away from the wound and landed in his lap. His head lolled back. The palm-leaf sombrero slipped off his filthy head and landed on the floor in a tinkling heap.

Longarm pushed his chair away from the poker table, then slipped his pistol back into its holster. He picked up the money he'd won and dropped it into the pocket of his suit coat.

A number of people crept from their hiding places behind the bar, and filtered over to stare at the oozing corpse. Someone relit the doused lamps.

The fancy-dressed gambler who'd been at the table when the disagreement flared up stood beside Longarm and said,

"My God, but you killed the hell out of 'im, didn't you, mister?"

Longarm cut a quick glance at the man, then said, "Well, friend, didn't really have much of a choice once he'd decided to draw down on me. It was either fight or die. Tried to talk him out of it, but as you surely heard, he wasn't havin' any of that. Far as I'm concerned, any alternative ending for this dustup would mean that I'd be dead right now. Better him than me."

Longarm turned to leave just as Manny Frazier strolled up. Frazier eyeballed the corpse. Shook his head. "Said you were gonna stir the pot some. Never figured on you goin' this far."

"Just worked out the way it worked out, Manny. Tried to get him to calm down. Didn't do any good. Went for his weapon. Left me no choice."

Frazier pulled his hat off and dropped it on the busted table. Ran his fingers through sweaty hair. "McCabe's gonna bust a gut when he hears about this. Jackasses he's been sendin' to shoot my jail up just might get serious next time out."

Longarm slapped the nervous city lawman on the shoulder. "Gotta keep pushin', Manny. Maybe McCabe'll do something he shouldn't, and we can throw his ass in a cell."

"Maybe. Wouldn't bet on it if I were you. Man's wicked to the core and slicker'n a dipper full of tadpoles. I fear you mighta just lit a fire under him we won't be able to put out till he's caused a lotta damage, Custis."

"You have any problems with the troublemaking Fowler McCabe, Manny, send for me. And I mean anything. He shows up in your office for another bitch rant, you send someone to find me as quick as you can. I'll put an end to such behavior right on the spot. Catch 'im spittin' on the boardwalk, call me. You wanna harass his evil old ass till he

126

gets tired of it and makes a mistake like the one our friend Millard Tubbs yonder made, send someone to find me."

Pecos's city marshal shook his head, then ran his fingers through his hair again. "Not very sportin' conduct on our part, Custis."

Longarm looked thoughtful for a few seconds before speaking again. "You know, Manny, there's just times when you have to bend the rules a mite to take dangerous people off the street and outta the lives of decent folks. Think this is one of those times. No longer'n I've been in town, seems McCabe's the logical suspect in almost every piece of criminal activity to occur around this town for years. Mail theft, murder, stock theft, land swindles, hell, you name it. And while he might be smarter'n a tree full a owls, and so evil he'd steal a widder woman's only milk cow, that don't mean we can't put a stop to his murderous, reprehensible ways. We'll push him and his people at every possible turn. Won't pass up a chance to bedevil the hell out of 'em. And by God, since I'm already here, that's exactly what I intend to do."

Chapter 14

Longarm pushed his way onto the boardwalk fronting the Palace Saloon. He elbowed through a cluster of clucking gawkers, but stopped long enough to scratch a match to life on a veranda support post and light a nickel cheroot. He stepped from beneath the covered porch and glanced at the sky. A near-full silvery moon had replaced that day's fiery, rust-colored sun.

Behind him, an inquisitive knot of nearly twenty of the curious, the concerned, and those with nothing more to do for entertainment milled about on the rugged boardwalk near the Palace's front entrance and in the street. They cussed, discussed, pointed, and loudly theorized on the deadly occurrence that had taken place prior to their arrival.

A barrel-gutted feller, sporting a tall-crowned hat big enough to sleep in, and a beard that looked like the blade of a much-used, long-handled shovel, held forth near the corner of one of the cantina's windows. "Well, by God, I got here right after the killin' happened, don't you know." He pointed into the saloon and shook his finger. "'At 'ere big feller over yonder in the chair musta pulled on the wrong man. 'Pears to me he's deader'n Santa Anna and headed for the ole stony lonesome."

A diminutive whiskey drummer who displayed all the physical characteristics of a human weasel stood with his suit coat pulled back, thumbs shoved into vest pockets, bowler hat tilted in a rakish fashion on the back of his head. "No doubt about it, you seem to have seen ever'thang that occurred, mister. By any chance did you manage to see who done the shootin'? By that I mean, who kilt the dead feller?"

Mr. Barrel Gut said, "No, sir. Didn't dare peek in till the shootin' were concluded. By then, whoever done him in had vacated the table, and I cannot say for certain sure which 'un of those as I can still see now might be the killer."

An anonymous voice in the crowd whimpered, "Sweet merciful Jesus, the dead feller's Millard Tubbs. He's one a Fowler McCabe's men." All of a sudden, the milling crowd fell silent, and then more than half of them made beelines for the darkest corners they could find.

Longarm ambled across the busy, dusty street and headed for the Orient Hotel. Suddenly, he felt tired to the bone and couldn't wait to try out that big soft bed in his room.

He'd taken but a few more steps when a swirling rush of movement came up behind him. His hand went to the grips of his pistol just as the beautiful Conchita slipped one of her arms into the crook of his.

The girl's beauty was even more spectacular in the soft glow of silver-tinted moonlight. She had draped a dark shawl over her head and formerly bare shoulders. The starkness of her face, framed by the covering, enhanced an innocence Longarm had not noticed in the saloon. There was something almost Biblical in her appearance.

With absolutely no preliminaries, she squeezed his arm, leaned close, and said, "You will take me to your room, Señor."

"That won't be necessary, Conchita."

"Oh, but you are wrong, Señor. You have saved my life tonight, and I feel compelled to show my . . ." She paused. "How you say it? A-a-a-pree . . . ?"

"Appreciation?"

"Sí. Yes. That is the word. My appreciation. Is no small thing you have done, Señor. Tubbs would have killed me had you not stopped him."

"Oh, perhaps not. In fact, I doubt it."

"You did not see his eyes, Señor. The flames of El Diablo burned there. I saw them. He has killed a number of others before tonight. When he grabbed my wrist, I felt sure my time had come. Had I been more careful of his mood, I would have known not to approach the crazed beast."

Never one to turn down an opportunity for an evening heavy with the possibility of unbridled lust with a woman such as the one clinging to his arm, Longarm led Conchita to the door of his second-floor hotel room. He stopped under the hall lamp and pulled the key from a vest pocket, but hesitated before entering. When he reached out and barely touched the knob, the door swung open on its own. Longarm took a quick step back and pulled his pistol.

Still clinging to his arm, Conchita pushed the shawl away from her face. "Is there a problem, Señor?"

"I'm not sure," he mumbled, then gently shoved the inquisitive girl to one side of the open portal. "Stay," he whispered, then eased across the threshold and into the deeper darkness of the room.

When a lamp in the room flickered to life, Conchita poked her head around the door facing. "Is okay to come inside now, Señor?"

Longarm stood beside the bed, the pistol still in hand. "Sure 'nuff, darlin'. Come right on in. Just that someone's been in my room since I left earlier this afternoon. Nothing

131

appears out of place, but I'd be willing to swear as how somebody's been in here."

Conchita appeared totally unconcerned with Longarm's housekeeping problems. She fetchingly flounced onto one corner of the thick mattress, then flopped over on her back. Her dress rode up above her knees and revealed a sweaty stretch of muscular upper thighs. She moaned, stretched, and arched her back, a pose designed to enhance her enormous breasts, and that raised her knee-length skirt even higher. She groaned, rubbed her thighs together, and the skirt fell to her waist, revealing a downy thatch of long, moist, ebony curls that appeared a perfect match for the hair on her head. Eyes slitted with smoldering lust, she rolled onto her side, yanked the blouse away from one of the massive orbs beneath, and began to fondle, pinch, and pull at its already stiffened nipple.

While still a bit preoccupied with the likelihood that someone might have entered his room, Longarm couldn't help but notice the near-naked girl squirming around on his bed. His attention became more firmly focused when she pushed both breasts upward, craned her neck forward, and sucked first one huge nipple, then the other. Back and forth her nibbling, sucking lips flew from one nipple to the other. At the same time she rubbed her glorious ass on the sheets and bedspread, then hunched the vacant air over her gaping, dewy snatch as though fucking some unseen but passionate lover.

Abruptly, one hand abandoned the breast it caressed, and dropped to the furry, pink-lipped, steaming treasure between her legs. At least three of her fingers dipped into the shiny stickiness. Longarm watched the girl give herself a vigorous fingering, before she jerked the sopping hand away, smelled her wet fingers, and licked away at the gooey nooky juice, one finger at a time. Then, when both hands dove into her steamy crotch, the girl's sex-charged whimpering got even more intense.

"Oh, *por favor, señor*," she mewled. "Conchita's *funci-ete es* on fire. *Está muy caliente*. I have wanted you inside me for hours. Please. Come to me now."

Longarm stumbled back to the door, threw the bolt, then propped a straight-backed chair against the knob. He ripped his clothing off as fast as he could. The suit coat and shirt ended up in a heap on top of the chest of drawers. His pants dangled by one leg from the back of a chair. Boots and socks were kicked into a messy pile in a corner next to the head of the bed.

Longarm stood totally naked beside the bed. He sported a hard-on that twanged like a bent handsaw being whacked with a hammer every time he touched it. He dropped his pistol belt onto the headboard for easy access should intruders enter during the festivities, and raised a knee, as though to climb into the bed. Before he could get himself atop the Mexican firecracker's gushing cooz, the fiesty Conchita twirled around, sat up on her knees, and grabbed his cock in both hands. She moaned, grunted, and made strange, incomprehensible sounds he'd never heard come from a woman before. Like a baby wildcat, she sucked on the portion of his enormous prod that spilled over what she already had in hand.

Longarm threw his head back and let the delicious enjoyment of the moment spread from his crotch to twitching toes that tried to scratch a hole in the colorful rug beneath his feet. He glanced back down into Conchita's mysterious dark eyes and realized she was watching him.

A smile appeared in the girl's eyes and played across her lips. She pulled away, licked the tip of his steely prong, then said, "You need not hold back, Señor. I know that some women do not like it in the mouth, but I harbor no such prejudice." She kissed and tongued the tip again. "Love it when *mi enamorado* comes in my mouth. In fact, I just love fucking in every form imaginable. Anything, done any way you can think of. And the more the better." Then she gobbled him down again and went back to sucking like something crazed.

Longarm closed his eyes, determined to simply take pleasure in her amazingly talented mouth and tongue. But after a few seconds, he realized she had abandoned his throbbing dick and appeared to be locked in an attempt to suck his balls completely off his body. That erotic maneuver certainly kicked the lid off.

Longarm grabbed the grinning Conchita by the shoulders and pushed her onto her back. He crawled between the randy girl's legs and shoved his massive love muscle into her scorching glory hole, until their pubic bones slapped against one another with a resounding plop.

The giggling chili pepper beneath him drew her legs up as far as she could. When it seemed as though she couldn't possibly get them any farther back, she used her elbows to push those shapely limbs to a point where both knees touched her ears. Then, as though totally new to the entire experience, she craned her neck forward. She stared, wide-eyed, at the noisy action going on at the center of her being, and appeared fascinated by the enormous staff of flesh sluicing in and out of her shuddering, gushing body.

In pretty short order, Longarm had built up a rapid, determined rhythm similar to that of the power rod on a Baldwin steam engine. Almost every second or third stroke of his muscular, pile-driving ass brought another effusive, noisy orgasm from the depths of little Conchita's very being.

A wave of passionate color surfaced in splotches beneath the girl's honey-colored skin. The entire upper half of her body turned a hot pink in color. Beads of glistening sweat appeared to burst from every viewable pore. Her toes curled into tight knots. Straightaway, both participants in the loud, aggressive lovemaking were covered in a slick, glowing, sheen that consisted of equal parts unbridled sex and steaming perspiration.

After what seemed nearly an hour of grunting and grinding, the tiny Conchita wrestled Longarm onto his back, then pinned him to soaking-wet sheets. She leaned back, a breast in each hand, and pinched her nipples so hard he marveled at the fact that they didn't bleed. Seemingly astride a wild, bucking mustang, she rode his enormous rod of love as though it might well be the last thing in this life she'd ever do. On a number of occasions she abruptly stopped, grabbed her frothy pussy with both hands, and let out a sound usually heard only by men fighting bloodthirsty Plains Indians to the death.

Just when Longarm thought the athletically gifted, insatiable girl had about worn his throbbing tool completely out, she twirled around with her back to him and went for an even wilder jaunt. A few minutes into the new position, she leaned as far forward as she could, while maintaining grinding contact with his cock. Longarm glanced down between them and watched, fascinated, as her fingers vigorously worked on his tool and her bouncing notch at the same time.

When he thought they had explored just about every imaginable position, she hopped off his quivering tool and draped her drenched, engorged quim over his face. Though his hearing was muffled by sweat-drenched legs, he did hear Conchita moaning, "Oh, *sí*, lick it. *Dios mio*. Lick it. Harder. Deeper. Use your tongue. Go deeper, Señor. Deeper."

After yodeling in the gulley for what felt like an hour, Longarm pushed the dripping girl off his face, flipped her onto her hands and knees, and slid his big banger back inside her. He reached around front with one hand and fingered her snatch until he found the most sensitive spot of her entire being, then grabbed a dangling tit and rolled the flint-hard nipple between a finger and thumb.

Conchita began to make sounds like a puppy yelping. Her frantic cries spurred Longarm to quicken an already furious pace. His frenzied efforts paid off when she fell forward on her face, then reached back between her legs and grabbed his balls. In a move that felt as though he was being milked, Conchita caressed him into a flurry of rapid-fire thrusts that ended in a thunderous, geyserlike orgasm that blew the still-hunching girl completely off the end of his pulsating cock.

Near exhaustion, Longarm leaned back and howled like the only wolf in the great cold and lonely. "Hot damn, girl," he yelped. And for just an instant, he imagined that the orgasmic crescendo that ended their first go-around of the evening was something akin to having a red-hot, flaming log chain yanked out of his ass.

For hours on end, they went at each other like wild animals. Once, he stood her against the wall and banged her until someone in the next room banged back and yelled, "For the love of God, give it a rest, folks. Shit. Not everyone in the world is havin' as much fun as you two."

Longarm laughed, then said, "Guess we'd best try to keep the noise down a bit, darlin'. Wouldn't want to get kicked out into the alley. Much more fun in here where there's a bed and, by God, a chair." With that, he marched across the room with the girl strapped around his waist, turned, and flopped into the waiting seat. Conchita immediately took the hint and rode him like the morning sun would never come up.

Between sessions Longarm sipped at a bottle of Maryland rye he kept in his possibles bag, and tried to dredge up something new and different to try with the voracious girl.

But no matter what he brought to mind, no matter how lasciviously delicious, including the time he opened a window and had her hang halfway out while he went at it from behind again, the insatiable Conchita had her own carnal preferences. She preferred bouts of end-to-end sucking and licking, and appeared totally unable to get enough.

At some point during one of those spirited you-lick-me-and-I'll-suck-you sessions, the exhausted lovers fell asleep—the girl on top, Longarm's root, nearly worn to the nub, still in her mouth.

The next thing he heard sounded like a ripping or tearing in the back of his sleep-benumbed brain. Someone was breaking the door down. He sat bolt upright in the bed, his face buried in Conchita's still-pulsating nookie, and grabbed for the pistol hanging from the headboard. The room thumped, roared like thunderation with gunfire, and lit up like midday on the Llano Estacado. Then a bottomless, black, purple-rimmed hole opened beneath the bed and swallowed him up, as surely as the whale got Jonah.

Chapter 15

A knife-edge of brain-penetrating light sliced through the darkness as Longarm groggily swam to the surface of heavy-headed consciousness. Muffled noise and movement shuffled back and forth and around him. The effort to open disinclined eyes proved an almost insurmountable task. Hours seemed to pass before he was finally able to force hesitant lids up far enough to see the face that loomed in front of him.

Marshal Manny Frazier leaned forward in his chair and held a cup of water to Longarm's rubbery lips. After several loud, slurping sips, Frazier drew the liquid away. "'Pears you're feelin' a bit better there, Custis. Had begun to wonder if'n you was ever gonna come out of it."

Longarm cast a bleary-eyed glance around the strange room, then pushed the heavy coverlet away and tried to swing his legs over the edge of the bed.

Frazier placed a steadying hand on the wounded man's shoulder and pushed him back. "Wouldn't try to get up just yet, my friend. You've been out for two days, almost three. Doc says it might take a spell for you to fully recover your senses. I expect he knows what he's talkin' about."

Longarm's unsteady fingers went to an intense, throbbing spot on the side of his head. Tenderly, he fingered at a long, matted, scab-covered gash just above his left ear. Patchy spots of dried blood flaked off the wound and dribbled onto his shoulder. He flicked the scabby chunks away, then twisted his neck back and forth.

"Sons a bitches damn near got you, Custis," Frazier observed. "Yep, you're a lucky feller, if'n I've ever known one. Look like one helluva a mess, but at least you're alive. 'Bout half an inch to the right and you'd be shovelin' coal in Satan's fiery pit, sure as the cow ate the cabbage."

"That's a pretty grim assessment, Manny. What makes you think I wouldn't be playin' a harp for St. Peter? Better yet, what the hell happened?"

"Playin' a harp? That's rich," Frazier snorted. "Way I found you, it's a wonder Ole Scratch don't have you in tow this very minute. You don't remember anything about what transpired? Nothin'?"

"Some. But it's cloudier'n Red River mud. Lord Almighty, my head throbs like a split watermelon." He started to check the wound again, but thought better of it. "Seems to me I was havin' the time of my life, and then the bottom fell out from under me, or the roof on me. Not sure which. Swear to Jesus, I ache all over like I've been jerked through a keyhole backward, then slapped nekkid and run over with a beer wagon."

Frazier nodded and smiled. "Well, you look every inch of that and then some. Near as I've been able to tell, somebody—maybe as many as three or four of 'em—kicked the door down and sprayed your hotel room with a swarm a blue whistlers. If you ain't the luckiest son of a bitch alive right now, I'd like to meet the man who is. Follow his ass around and start copyin' whatever in hell he's a-doin'."

All of a sudden, the reality of the situation came flooding back in snatches of color, noise, gun smoke, blood, and screaming. "The girl. Damn. Can't remember her name. She all right?"

"Sorry, Custis. She didn't make it. When I arrived on the scene, she was lying on top of you—shot full of holes. You were out cold with that nasty crease in your noggin, and at first everybody thought sure you was dead, too. Sure as hell looked dead. Mess a blood all over you just mighta saved your life. Once we realized our mistake, I got you moved outta there as quick as I could. Scooped up all your traps and such. Put you up in the jail at first."

Longarm closed his eyes and pinched the bridge of his nose, then waved a hand at the room and said, "Jail? Where the hell am I now? This sure as shootin' ain't your jail, and it ain't my hotel room."

"You're in one of the bedrooms on the upper floor of Clegg's Store. Soon as Constance Parker found out about what had befallen your poor, poor, pitiable ass, she insisted I move you up here. All around, figure it's probably the best thing. Spirited you over here in the middle a the night so's no one would know where you'd been situated. Gotta tell ya, Custis, 'pears to me as how no longer'n you've been in town, you've done managed to really rub ole Fowler McCabe's rhubarb the wrong way."

"Think he's behind this, do you?"

"Oh, hell, yes, and that attempted ambush in my doorway, too. Originally thought that little dustup was nothin' more'n an effort to send me a message to mind my own business, but I done gone and rethunk that 'un. Buckin' Fowler McCabe, and blowing Cooch Smeed's thumb off first jump outta the box, musta put a bug the size of a washtub up McCabe's ass."

Longarm's head lolled back into the enormous feather pillow propping him up. "Cooch Smeed? Was that his name?

From the way McCabe told it, the stupid bastard was some kinda famous gunman. Never even heard of Cooch Smeed." As though suddenly struck by the thought, he scratched his chin, then shook his head. "Christ, Manny. Does Constance know *how* you found me? I mean, does she know—?"

"Don't worry. Took care of the whole shebang. Hushed everything up from the get-go. Anyone from the Orient, or as helped me with the move, opens his mouth, they'll have to answer to me."

"What about the girl? Conchita, wasn't it?"

"Had no family or other ties around Pecos. None I've been able to pin down anyways. 'Pears to be just another dirt-poor gal a-tryin' to make her way in a rough-and-tumble world. Worked for whatever she could pick up at the Palace and a couple a other saloons here in town."

"That it?"

"Not really. She appeared to spend a lot of time at the Gem—place favored by McCabe's men. Near as I can tell, she hadn't been in town but a few weeks. Just one of those poor souls who happened to be in the wrong place at the wrong time. Over the years, I've come of the opinion that life's nothin' more'n an accident and sometimes so's death."

Longarm shook his head back and forth like an old dog looking for a place to lie down. "Guess you took care of the arrangements for her as well?"

"Yes. Indeed I did. Attended the service myself. Local undertaker did a fine job. Kept it quiet, of course. Doubt anyone in town's even missed her yet."

"Wouldn't bet on that one, Manny."

"Buried a box full of rocks with your name on it right beside her. Now everyone in town thinks you've done give up your guitar and headed for the last roundup."

A tentative smile creaked across Longarm's haggard

face. "You know, I've been a lot of things in this life, Manny. First time I can remember ever bein' dead and buried."

In a flurry of distinctly feminine sounds and smells, Constance Parker bustled into the room and headed to Longarm's side. She caressed his brow, then took his hand in hers and smiled. "Well. Thought I could hear you men talking. So pleased to see you've come back to us, Marshal Long. We've all been very concerned."

Struck by the woman's startling, flaxen-haired beauty and obvious distress, Longarm pushed his way up against a heaping mound of pillows. He tried his best to convey the appearance of a man rapidly regaining strength and prowess.

"Just give me a few minutes to clear my head, Miss Parker, and I'll be up and about plenty pronto. Be dancin' 'round this bed 'fore you know it."

"You'll do no such thing, Custis Long. You'll take your time and properly recover from this terrible injury. I'm but a few steps away, as I have been since your arrival. Well, except for the day I took the time to visit Uncle Frank's final resting place. Anyway, I'll be at your beck and call until you are completely restored. Even at night. My bedroom is just next door. Now, what can I get for you?"

Longarm rubbed his stomach. "Have to admit, I am a bit on the hungry side."

Constance brightened up and smiled. "Well, given you've had nothing to eat for several days, I would expect that you might be famished. How does coffee, six eggs, some biscuits covered in pepper gravy, and a slab of bacon sound to you?"

"So empty I could eat the blades off a windmill right now. Figure a breakfast like that'd be just dandy, Miss Constance. Just dandy."

"Fine, I'll go see to your meal, and you gentlemen can

go back to your conversation. I'm certain Marshal Frazier has a plethora of questions about the men who did this horrible thing to you."

The nose-tingling aroma of magnolias still hung in the air around Longarm's head after Constance had nodded to her wounded guest and then bowed out of the room. "Quite a woman, ain't she, Manny," he said.

"Indeed. Opened this place up within an hour after you ran McCabe off. Put all her uncle's clerks back to work. Whole bunch a happy folks here in town 'cause a that lady. 'Course, she's really pissed McCabe off even more than usual. Man's so mad, the pupils of his eyes is pulled up like number-nine bird shot."

"Well, fuck him and the horse he rides, too."

"Was lookin' out your window a few minutes 'fore you came around. Spotted the back-shootin' scum 'cross the street yonder with Dorsey Barber. Kep' lookin' over this way and pointin'. Both of 'em look like they've got their hats set at a fightin' angle."

"Orpheus Stonehouse hasn't shown his face yet?"

"Not as I'm aware of. But, hell, that double-evil skunk could be slinkin' around behind the scenes somewheres and I wouldn't know it."

Longarm groaned, closed his eyes, and pulled the cover back up around his chin. "You don't mind, Manny, think I'll take a little nap. Gonna try to look as pitiful as possible when Constance comes back with my meal. Figure the more pathetic I am, the more attention I'll get."

Frazier snorted like a winded horse, stood, stuffed his hat on, and started for the door. He stopped with a hand on the knob and glanced back at his injured friend. "So far, McCabe ain't aware that you're up here and still kickin', Custis. Don't know how long I can keep him from findin' out the truth. Best stay away from the windows until you're at least feelin' up to speed. Bet my next month's pay, soon as he ferrets out the truth of the cheat we're playin' on him, you're gonna be knee-deep in Dorsey Barber, or Orpheus Stonehouse, or maybe both of 'em."

For nigh on a week, Longarm allowed himself the pleasant indulgence of Constance Parker's constant comfort and soft-glove care. During the course of five glorious days of honing his pitiful act, she helped him from the bed, saw to his twa-let by shaving his stubble-covered face, changed his bed and clothing every morning, twice gave him a sponge bath, fed him like a king, sat up nights reading to him, and on a number of occasions even helped him downstairs to the indoor privy—an extravagant convenience rarely seen in places as far off the beaten path as Pecos.

But on the sixth morning, after a fine breakfast of flapjacks, eggs, bacon, and sausage, he decided it was about time to gut up, get off his dead ass, and face the world. He dressed himself, and had just gotten armed when a noisy commotion from the downstairs area of the store caught his attention. He tiptoed to the second-floor landing and cocked an inquisitive ear onto the situation developing below.

From the direction of the counter, on the opposite side of the building, he heard a clearly agitated Constance Parker say, "I'll thank you to take your thugs and leave my place of business, Mr. McCabe. They've damaged property and goods, which I fully expect you to pay for."

Longarm checked the Colt to make sure it was primed, lying in the holster properly, and ready for action, then took a single step down the staircase and toward the noisy dispute. Something heavy hit the floor with a resounding thump that sent a shuddering wave all the way up to the first tread at the top of the stairway.

Longarm could tell, from the ebb and flow of the conversation, that Constance was behind the glass-fronted counter on his right when she said, "That's a hand-tooled saddle and has a price tag of forty dollars on it, Mr. McCabe. If your man has damaged it in any way whatsoever, the price will be added to a bill I'm tallying for you at this very instant."

Near the front entrance, Longarm heard the oily voice of Fowler McCabe when he snarled, "Three times now I've gone and offered you a fair price for this place. Figure you best take it, woman, or my men might be forced to get even more destructive 'fore we leave."

One stealthy step at a time, Longarm moved down and closer to the noisy action. Eventually, he was able to see McCabe and his two henchmen. One of them was the fat slug from his first encounter with Pecos's most belligerent citizen. The trio had their collective attention so focused on tormenting Constance, and a weeping clerk who hovered by her side, that none of them even noticed when Longarm hit the bottom step of the stairs and silently eased onto the first-floor landing.

All three of Constance's persecutors jumped as though they'd been shot when Longarm said, "You know, McCabe, seems like we've already done this dance before. Last time 'round, that ugly tub a guts doin' your dirty work lost a thumb durin' the disagreement. Which one a these idgets accompanyin' you today is gonna make the mistake of a lifetime?"

McCabe snapped a wicked, teeth-grinding glance in Longarm's direction. Bluish veins under the gray skin of his neck and temple bulged and throbbed. For an instant, Longarm would have sworn the man looked as though someone had slapped him across the face—hard.

"Well, I'll just be royally damned," McCabe muttered. "If you ain't a sight to behold. A walkin', by God, bullet-riddled corpse."

The stunned reaction to a dead man's reappearance didn't last anywhere nearly as long as Longarm had hoped. McCabe recovered in record time, then made an imperceptible waving motion with one pale, bloodless hand.

A third man Longarm had somehow failed to notice appeared as though he'd risen up through the cracks in the dusty floor. Like some sort of miasmic, ghoulish mist found only in penny dreadfuls filled with phantasmagoric tales of ghosts, ghouls, and grave robbers, the grisly-looking gunman oozed across the floor like a disease-carrying fog. He stopped a step behind McCabe and fixed unblinking yellow eyes on his prey. To Longarm's distinct discomfort, an air of tangible tension suddenly took on the aspect of a possible life-and-death encounter.

Chapter 16

A look of smoldering evil flashed across McCabe's gaunt face when he said, "Very impressed with your stunning resurrection, given as how everyone in town figured you for a dead man. Gonna have to go by and compliment Marshal Frazier for the dodge. Extraordinary cheat he's gone and put over on everyone, I must admit."

Longarm grinned. "Oh, not that much of a trick really. 'Specially when you consider the audience."

Blood rose in McCabe's pale cheeks. "Well, now, that's just much too modest of you. This here's just about the most amazing thing I've witnessed since the time a traveling conjurer came through town and caught a bullet with his teeth. Hell, I even stopped at the Mount Olive Cemetery for a few minutes the other day and viewed your hand-carved tombstone myself. Right impressive. Yessir, impressive, to say the very least."

Longarm flipped the tail of his coat away from the Colt. "Couldn't have been that you just wanted to make sure your men had done their jobs, could it?"

McCabe offered up a flat-eyed, reptilian smile. "Why, I

never said nothin' like that, Marshal. Surprised and disappointed that you'd make such an inflammatory statement."

"Breaks my heart that you're so insulted."

McCabe shrugged the challenge off. "So far our only disagreement seems to be over the ownership of this one piece of property. Figure we should be able to settle any questions about how I feel on this particular matter right here today. 'Course, in the end, you might not care for the outcome. Oh, like you to make the acquaintance of Dorsey Barber, Marshal Long. I'm sure he's as impressed with your dramatic recovery as I am."

Barber strutted up to stand beside his funereal-looking boss. On the gunman's heavy silver spurs, Mexican rowels the size of ten-dollar gold pieces made musical, tinkling sounds against dangling, shank-mounted jingle bobs. Lean as a strip of chewed rawhide, draped in black that was high lighted with polished silver from hand-tooled toe to flat-brimmed crown, the sullen gunman snatched the stub of a chewed cheroot from between thin, cruel lips and flicked it onto the floor. The butts of matched, bone-gripped Remington pistols, worn in the contrary Wild Bill Hickok fashion, twinkled at Longarm like the blinking eyes of hungry predators on the prowl.

In a voice that sounded like a starved wolf growling from the bottom of an open grave, Barber snarled, "Never even heard of you till you was supposed to be dead, Long. Then, all of a sudden, seemed like the whole fuckin' town was a-tellin' all these wild-assed, heroic tales 'bout that *famed* Deputy U.S. Marshal Custis Long." He waved an arm, as though speaking to a huge throng of people. "Bold law bringer known all over the West for his deadly pistoleering skills, manly good deeds, service to the downtrodden, and, of course, prowess with the ladies."

In a tone tinted with false humility, Longarm said, "Oh,

I wouldn't go quite that far. Bold law bringer, yeah. But all that other stuff is just rumor and the kinda idle speculation typical of the ignorant and ill informed."

Barber picked at a spot on a chapped, cracked lip and then rubbed something on the front of his wine-colored, silk vest. He examined the end of his finger, then added, "Gotta say, Long, I agree with yer own personal assessment. You don't look like much to me. Figure I can take you down a peg or two and not even work up a sweat."

Longarm slanted a quick glance from one of McCabe's secondary gunmen to the other and then back to Barber. Of the three, Barber was beyond any doubt the man to reckon with. But the way Longarm had it figured, if Barber proved stupid enough to go for one of his fancy, bone-gripped pistols, all three of McCabe's gunnies would have to be put down, and as quickly as possible.

The prospect that Constance and her terrified clerk might get caught up in an all-guns-a-blazing firefight flitted across the back of Longarm's brain. Just as quickly, he shoved the thought aside with the realization that survival might well be the next order of business inside Clegg's Mercantile.

Rather than grant Barber anything like the least bit of respect, Longarm ignored the man and spat back, "Look, McCabe, think it best you take your lapdogs and head for the street. Get on back down to your own shop and leave Miss Parker alone. 'Course, if that don't quite suit your purpose here today, I'll be glad to follow all of you to the street and we can settle any problems you have out there. Can't answer for you, of course, but I wouldn't want any lead to start flying inside the store while we have two innocent female bystanders present."

To everyone's obvious shock and surprise, Constance Parker reached under the counter she stood behind and came up with a sawed-off ten-gauge coach gun. From Longarm's

151

vantage point, it appeared she brought the big-barreled Greener to bear right on Fowler McCabe's crotch. The weepy, red-eyed clerk took shelter behind her boss and looked frightened slap to death.

"Don't concern yourself about us, Marshal Long," Constance said without taking her eyes off McCabe. "I think my uncle's favorite weapon should just about equalize this vexing situation a bit."

McCabe tilted his head like an inquisitive animal and made a tentative, imploring motion with one hand. "Do be careful with that thing, Miss Parker. Slip of the finger could destroy everyone in front of you."

"You think I'm just a stupid woman and don't know that, Mr. McCabe? Be fully aware that if any of your men make the slightest move for their weapons, I'll be most happy to send the whole bunch of you on a Heavenly path straightaway and to a much-deserved meeting with blessed Jesus. You'll be the first to go."

With an apprehensive shushing motion of both hands, McCabe said, "Now, now. No need to get any more agitated than you already are, Miss Parker."

"You haven't seen agitated yet, sir. Given the firepower I'm holding, and how close we're standing to one another, if you or your men continue with your quarrelsome behavior and force me to fire, I doubt there'll be enough of the four of you left to sweep up on a dustpan once the smoke clears."

While it was a bold statement for a woman, the grit in her voice left no doubt in Longarm's mind that Constance Parker meant every word.

With that, the resolute girl cocked both hammers back on the big boomer. The grinding, metallic clicks sounded like somebody cracking walnuts on the countertop with a ball-peen hammer. McCabe, Barber, and the other two gunmen froze in place as though a blue norther had just blown through the front door from Montana and deposited a foot-thick layer of clear ice on every living thing in Texas.

All of a sudden, McCabe appeared to get a serious dose of soul-searching, heartfelt, apologetic religion. A pale, bloodless hand shot out and plucked at Dorsey Barber's elbow. "Wait. Wait now. No need for bloodshed. Just tryin' to conduct a little business here, that's all. Never expected anything like the turn of events as they now stand."

Longarm almost burst out laughing. "I'll bet you didn't. Bet you figured on steamrollin' this lady into whatever in hell you had in mind."

Constance refused to let McCabe off that easy. She raised the shotgun to her shoulder and aimed directly at his head. "You call bringing your bunch of clumsy toadies in here to damage my property and goods, in an attempt to intimidate me, nothing more than 'conducting a little business'? I think you'd best head for the nearest church, Mr. McCabe. Spend a bit of time talking with the Maker. Ask forgiveness for your lying, abusive nature. Perhaps our Lord and Father will see fit to bestow a divine visit upon you and change some of the hardhanded, hard-hearted ways you tend to use on your fellow men and what you obviously perceive as defenseless women."

McCabe let out a low, nervous, cackling chuckle, pulled at Barber's sleeve again, and motioned him back. Barber, along with the two other thugs, took a retreating step toward the open front door, but looked angry, confused, and more than a little agitated.

"Perhaps you're right, Miss Parker," McCabe offered. "In my overzealous eagerness to have a definitive decision from you, in regard to selling this property to me, perhaps I've been a bit too impatient. I do hope you'll accept my humble apology."

153

McCabe couldn't take his eyes off the enormous, open barrels of Constance Parker's shotgun, even when Longarm said, "Lady says your men damaged some of her valuable merchandise. Destroyed goods and such. Heard considerable destructive-sounding racket on my way down the stairs just now. I imagine that Miss Parker would be most grateful if you offered to make restitution for that damage. How much you think this buncha snakes owes you for their ham-fisted misbehavior, Miss Parker?"

Constance didn't miss a beat. "If we ignore the saddle they just knocked over, thirty dollars ought to just about cover their awkwardness and folly."

McCabe made a tentative move toward the inside pocket of his black, swallow-tailed coat. He stopped short, shrugged, and said, "May I reach inside, Miss Parker? Please be assured that I do not carry a weapon of any kind and would hate to be shot dead by mistake."

Constance nodded her approval, but the ten-gauge blaster remained trained on her rival's viperlike head.

Clasping it between two fingers, McCabe carefully extracted a fancy leather wallet from his coat pocket. With a great deal of sneering, officious ceremony, he removed three ten-dollar notes and laid them atop the nearest glass case. "That should take care of any *accidental* damage my boys might have inadvertently caused, Miss Parker. If not, simply make a list, at your convenience of course, and see I get it as soon as possible. And now, if you'll lower that man-killin' shoulder cannon of yours, we'll be on our way."

Dripping with sarcasm, Constance replied, "Do pardon the inconvenience, Mr. McCabe, but I won't lower my weapon, and you will take your groveling toadies and leave—immediately."

The nail-biting situation appeared on the verge of being diffused up to that point. But even as he backed toward the door, Barber sneered, then shook a finger at Constance and growled, "What the hell did you jus' call me, woman? A *toady*?" Then he glanced at McCabe as if looking for clarification. "What the hell's a *toady*, Fowler? Woman done went and called me a name I don't even understand, for Christ's sake. Cain't nobody be a-callin' me stuff like a *toady*, by God. I've kilt folks for less."

Barely loud enough to be heard, Longarm said, "Aw, shut the hell up, you son of a bitch. Keep runnin' your stupid mouth and you just might get called a helluva lot worse than a toady. I start callin' you names, and you can bet you'll understand exactly what I mean."

At the door, Barber made a move like he intended to come back inside. McCabe grabbed the angry gunman by the arm and pulled him onto the boardwalk with the other two henchmen. "Let it go," McCabe kept saying. "Let it go. There'll be another time. Trust me, there'll be another time."

The argument over exactly what a toady might be continued just outside the main entrance to Clegg's Mercantile, and got louder and more heated. Barber's agitation appeared to grow rather than diminish as McCabe pushed him away from the scene of their most recent effort at threatening coercion.

Longarm watched the quartet through the store's front window as they stood on the boardwalk, ranted, waved their arms, and cursed all and sundry. Then he marched over to the counter, made a gimme motion with one hand, and said, "The shotgun, Constance. Lemme have it 'fore you touch the big popper off and destroy everything in the store."

Reluctantly, she handed the heavy weapon over, shrugged, and said, "What do I do now?"

Longarm carefully let the hammers down on the shotgun, then laid the weapon over his arm. "Take the young lady with you and get upstairs."

"You'll have to think of something other than that, Marshal Long. Personally, I feel strongly that I should stay here and help you."

Longarm gritted his teeth and shook his head. "And what, exactly, would you do, Constance?"

"Whatever it takes. I'm not afraid of McCabe and that bunch of thugs of his," she said, then reached under the counter and came up with a brace of Smith & Wesson Schofield pistols.

"Good Lord, woman, how many weapons have you got hid under there?"

She flashed an angelic smile. "Enough to take care of louts like those still standing on the veranda outside and blocking entry to my front door. Made up my mind the day Marshal Frazier brought you back here injured that I would not allow men of McCabe's ilk to use their power to threaten me again."

"Sounded as though he was well on the way to doing exactly that right before I made my way downstairs. Near as I could tell, you weren't doin' yourself any good a'tall arguing with the man over broken merchandise. Situation was bad and on the way to gettin' a lot worse, if you want my humble opinion on the subject."

"Well, that might have seemed the case to a man of action such as yourself," she sniffed. "But believe me, Marshal Long, I had the situation well in hand. If McCabe's men had gone any further in their belligerent behavior, my uncle's Greener would most certainly have made its appearance earlier and helped that belligerent bunch in their efforts to reconsider such aberrant conduct."

Longarm shrugged and, shotgun still draped across his arm, headed for the door. "Well, then, do what you think best, Constance. I'll trail McCabe and his crew just to make sure

156

they're well away from here, then stop in and report all this to Marshal Frazier." He stood in the open doorway long enough to add, "Do be careful, though. Wouldn't want to come back and find you'd shot yourself, or your pretty helper."

Easing onto the boardwalk, he spotted McCabe, Barber, and the others, but stayed well behind them and kept a sharp eye on their actions. Men, women, and children were rudely pushed from their path as the quartet plowed along four abreast until they reached McCabe's huge but nearly deserted emporium and disappeared inside.

Longarm stepped off the walkway in front of a busy Chinese laundry, then picked a dusty path across the crowded thoroughfare and headed for the Orient Hotel. Once inside the lobby, he found a spot to sit near the inn's huge, sparkling-clean, beveled-glass window—a place where he could discreetly observe all the comings and goings directly across the street at McCabe's.

After nearly an hour of unblinking, mind-numbing study on the subject, he stopped a passing waiter and ordered a tumbler of Maryland rye from the hotel's bar. He settled himself in for what appeared as though it was about to turn into a long day of the most boring kind of work for any lawman. Waiting was the one part of his job that the veteran deputy U.S. marshal openly despised.

Two sips into his drink, a rider who looked more like a working brush popper than a gunman fogged up to McCabe's Emporium on a well-lathered dun horse, then leaped from his animal and hurried inside. Within seconds, the stranger, McCabe, Barber, and the two men who'd accompanied McCabe and Barber most recently in their visit to Constance Parker stormed into the street. They got mounted in a rush, kicked their animals west, and fogged out of town in a dust-slinging cloud.

Longarm tossed his drink down, snatched the shotgun up, and headed for Manny Frazier's office. He couldn't imagine what might be going on, but didn't like what he'd just seen. Nope, not one little bit.

Chapter 17

Damage to the front of Frazier's office and jail had been repaired with fresh lumber, and the front window replaced with a set of weighty, iron-bound shutters. Longarm pushed the door open and stepped inside. A wizened, toothless scarecrow of a man, who looked like the Dead Sea wasn't even feeling sick when his mama pushed him into the world, dragged a damp mop around on the office floor and made sounds like he might pass out.

"Where's Marshal Frazier, old-timer?" Longarm asked.

The geezer stopped swabbing at the rough planks long enough to lean on his mop handle, scratch a stubble-covered, toothless jaw, then paw at the greasy, ill-kept wad of hair on his head and mumble, "Name's Pike. Waldo Pike. And, well, seems as how he done said somethin' 'bout goin' out to help Sheriff Miller with some horse thievin', or some such. Called it 'county business' as I recall. Does that a lot, you know. Lotta county business 'round here."

"You a deputy?"

The codger let out a rueful chuckle. "No, I'm a practicin' drunk. Damn good 'un, too. Borderline professional. Should be licensed and bonded."

"That a fact. Well, Mr. Pike, Waldo, did Manny say when he'd be back?"

Pike went through his whole scratching routine again before he stared at the ceiling for several seconds, then said, "Nope. Cain't say as how he did. Not sure when he'll be comin' on back, mister. Been gone since day 'fore yestiddy, or maybe longer. Two, three days. Hear tell they's lots a horse thievery goin' on out in the county."

Longarm propped Constance's shotgun against the wall, then fished a piece of paper and a stubby pencil from his coat pocket. Before he could start his note, a sweat-stained, grime-covered Manny Frazier burst through the door, tromped over to his desk, and threw a Winchester rifle onto it. He snatched his hat off and beat a swirling cloud of fine dust off his shirt and breeches.

The grizzled old fogy went back to pushing his mop again, then said, "Well, 'pears as how he's back, mister. Somewhat unexpected, but he's back."

With a roiling veil of grit swirling around him, Frazier said, "Damn, Waldo, you're gonna mop a hole right through the floor if you don't give it a rest."

An expression of pain hit Pike's face. "Ain't got nothin' else to do, Manny. You know that. 'Sides, don't matter how much I mop this place, it still stays dirtier'n the inside of a stable. You're lucky I ain't got nothin' else to do but drink and mop your floor when I'm sober."

"Yeah, yeah, yeah. I know, Waldo." Frazier patted the old man on the shoulder, then flopped into his squeaky chair and ran dirty fingers through sweat-drenched hair. Sounding tired and damn near wrung out, he said, "What's up, Custis?"

The paper and pencil went back in his coat pocket as Longarm said, "Looks to me like you've got an axle draggin' in the dirt, Manny. Your ass gets any lower, you're gonna rub a hole in your britches."

"True enough. I'm tired right to the bone. Been chasin' horse thieves all over Reeves County for the past two, aw, hell, might as well say three days. Damn near ever since I last saw you. Sons a bitches been stealin' anythin' that ain't nailed down or padlocked to a tree. Need to build a damned high fence around your property if'n you've got Fowler McCabe for a neighbor."

"Catch any of 'em?"

Frazier pulled his bottle of gold-labeled rye from the desk and poured two glasses. He shoved one of the tumblers Longarm's direction, then took a healthy swig from his own before saying, "Damn sure did. Sheriff Bud Miller got up a posse of real hard cases and found us a helluva tracker."

"Bet the hoople-heads figured it was about time."

"Yeah, well, 'pears ole Bud did finally run outta patience with all the complaints from the small ranchers hereabouts. Think they've just about gnawed his entire ass off one little-bitty chunk at a time. We always knew pretty much where them thievin' skunks was to start with, but just hadn't been able to pin 'em down."

Longarm took a sip of his drink, smacked liquor-dampened lips, shook his head, then sat down in the chair against the wall. "Well, if you caught some of 'em, where are they?"

"Left 'em in the big cold and lonely, where all horse thieves should end up. Way it all shook out, we just got plain lucky. Happened to come up on half a dozen of the sons a bitches tryin' to run some stock off'n a ranch 'tween here and Toya. Not really all that far outta town. 'Course they panicked and started shootin'. We kilt the hell outta four of 'em in a runnin' gun battle on the way back to their camp. Sneaky bastards had a buncha rope pens built in a box canyon I couldna found with a compass, a telescope, a sextant, and a good bloodhound."

"What happened to the other two?"

"Bit a seriously applied cow-pasture justice, Custis. Both of 'em had runnin' irons tied to their saddles. Too dim-witted to dump 'em, I guess. You know how folks in this part of the country feel about runnin' irons. Found a half-decent tree and strung 'em up." Frazier hesitated for a second in his tale-telling, then flashed a grim smile. "Be willin' to bet ole McCabe's gonna be damned upset when he finds out about the whole dance, too. Musta wiped out near half his crew."

"Sure the men you and Miller caught were McCabe's?"

"No way to prove it, a course, but I'd bet my next three months pay they spent most a their time workin' at his Bar M ranch, eatin' his food, and chewin' off'n his plug. Also be willin' to follow that bet with one on how pissed off ole Mc-Cabe's gonna be when he finds out how we just made one helluva dent in all a his horse stealin' enterprises. Probably send one or two a his gun thugs over here to personally make arrangements for me to catch a sunbeam straight to Heaven."

With the geezer mopping around his feet, Longarm saluted Frazier with his empty glass. "No need to wait on that wager. Think McCabe already knows all about what happened."

A quizzical look flashed across the haggard town marshal's face. "How you figure that one, Custis? Hell, I just told you. No one else in town knows. 'Cept Waldo here, and he ain't gonna tell nobody."

"Well, earlier this morning, I caught McCabe and some of his boys tryin' to hand Constance Parker a rasher a steamin' shit."

"Man has no shame, conscience, or understanding of

gentlemanly conduct, that's for sure. And he's a horse thief on top a that."

"Anyhow, I followed 'em to McCabe's store. Watched the front of the place for about an hour or so 'fore a feller that looked like a professional leather-pounder tore up and ran inside. Bet he wasn't there much more'n a minute when all of 'em came stormin' out, got mounted, and headed west."

Frazier pushed his chair away from the desk and stood. He tossed back the remains of his drink, then smacked the glass down on top of his desk. "Damn well better believe he'll be comin' back. And sooner rather than later. Man rarely stays away from his store for more'n an hour at a time. Gonna be *muy* pissed off, too."

"Yeah, well let 'im be pissed. Ain't gonna hurt my feelin's none."

"Before he discovers what has transpired and makes the turnaround, Custis, I'm goin' next door to Wong's Bath House and sit in a tub a clean, hot water for about an hour. None a them seconds or thirds for me either. Nossir. Gonna be the first one in the tub for a change. Cost me a dollar, but it'll be worth it."

"Don't blame you, Manny. You smell like a bouquet a West Texas stinkweed the size of a wagon wheel."

Frazier snatched his hat up and stuffed it on his sweaty head. "Well, fuck you, too, Marshal Custis Long. I ain't been so lucky lately that I've had the most beautiful woman in town a-bathin' me, shavin' my face, and seein' to my every need for the past four days. Some guys just got all the fuckin' luck," he said, then started for the door.

Pike trailed behind, mopping after every step.

"You feel safe gettin' nekkid, chuckin' your pistol, and climbin' into a tub of soapy water?" Longarm asked. "Sounds to me like you'd be the by-God perfect example of a sittin' duck."

Frazier stopped in the doorway with a hand on the brass knob. "Well, sure you probably remember as how I used to have a buncha deputies to kinda follow me around and watch out for me. And you know the way that story ends."

"Tell you what, Manny, I got nothin' else to do right now. Let me take this here big boomin' man-killer of Constance's and sit outside the door for you. Make sure McCabe or Dorsey Barber don't sneak up and kill the hell out of you while you're scrubbin' your nasty ass with bath oils and soap-scented water."

Frazier forced a pained smile, then turned to the aged mop pusher. "You sleepin' in one a the cells tonight, Waldo?"

"Well, you know me, Manny. It's either here or the alley behind the Palace. Old drunks don't have all that many choices in this life. Our options have a tendency to kinda narrow up on us."

"You can stay in here with me tonight. I'm gonna den up in one of the cells myself. Figure, if'n I should go to sleep in my own bed, someone's likely to slip in and murder me during my dreams. Same way they killed Frank Clegg."

Longarm followed Frazier onto the street and walked with him past V.W. Cramp's Variety Store and the Brewster Hotel. Brewster's beveled window revealed a carpeted lobby with tables, overstuffed chairs, and brass spittoons.

"'S a right nice-lookin' hotel," Longarm offered as they strolled past. "Guess I shoulda strolled on down this way. Woulda been closer to your office, Manny."

"Yeah. 'S where I have a room. Closest place to the office, that's for sure. Easy walk in the mornin's. Had me a woman for a spell right after I got here. We thought about buyin' a house, but then she up and run off to Kansas City with a drummer what sold ladies' undergarments."

"Ladies' undergarments? Be damned. Seems like a man

can make a living doin' just about anything these days, don't it?"

"I suppose. But you know, Custis, that snaky son of a bitch got her to the big city and turned her out to whore for 'im. Poor girl didn't have any more sense than a blind goose about such a life. One a her customers beat her to death a month later out behind a Wyoming Street saloon. Still pisses me off just to think about it."

Long watched as a weary, dejected Manny Frazier fumbled his way into Wong's Bath House. Man looked like he'd been run down, run over, and wrung out.

Soon as the door closed behind his beaten-down friend, Longarm flopped onto a boardwalk bench and stretched out. A thick bank of clouds had come up out of the west at some point earlier in the day and managed to cool everything off a mite. The blazing sun, which would normally have bored a hole in a man's head, was nowhere to be seen, and the unmoving bank of clouds overhead appeared on the verge of opening up and inundating the whole town.

He pulled a cheroot, fired a match, and puffed the smoke to life. Tipped his hat down over his eyes so he could watch passersby without being noticed. About halfway through the stogie, he'd relaxed so much he found it hard to hold his head up. Then Fowler McCabe and his bunch came thundering back in and that perked him up right smart.

He stood and moved to the edge of the boardwalk and, with concentrated intensity, watched as the same four men he'd buffaloed in Clegg's reined their animals up in front of McCabe's place and stormed inside. The look on McCabe's gaunt face could've frightened children, scared impressionable women, and poisoned well water.

Longarm slumped back onto the bench. *Probably don't*

mean mucha nothin', he thought. After another mind-numbing spell of inactivity, he napped off and had a fleeting, strange dream about Constance Parker. Seemed as though he could see the girl's face at the bottom of a sulfurous pit and that she called out to him for help.

He snapped awake as though someone had slapped him across the face and he didn't know why. The smoldering cheroot had gone out between his fingers. He slipped the Ingersoll watch from the pocket of his vest and snapped the cover open. More than an hour had passed. Off on the horizon, a bloodred sun peeked from beneath the darkening cloud cover like a burning lump of coal under a blanket.

All of a sudden, the yawning lawdog caught a muffled, popping sound off in the distance that snapped his head around and snatched him to his feet. Gotta be gunfire, he thought, but muted, barely discernible above all of the racket generated by movement in the crowded thoroughfare.

He stood, gazed as far down the street toward Clegg's as he could, and noticed people running. It was never a good sign when people started running, because they were generally running away from something—and most times that was frequently death.

He hopped into the street just as Manny Frazier burst from Wong's doorway all cleaned up, shaved, refreshed, and smiling. Soon as the city lawman, now scrubbed pink, noticed the alarm on Longarm's face, his toothy grin bled away.

Frazier slipped an arm into his leather vest and peered along the street with his friend. "What's the problem, Custis? Look like somebody just walked over your grave," he said.

Eyebrows pinched together over the bridge of his nose, Longarm stared into the dying sunlight and pointed with his free hand. "There. See? Back down at the other end of the street. Gotta be more'n a hundred yards away and hard to see, but looks to me like people scatterin' as though they're tryin' to get away from something near Clegg's. Thought I heard gunfire earlier, but it was . . ." He hesitated, scratched the back of his neck, then said, "Don't know if it means anything, but I saw McCabe and his boys come back just like you said they would. Jesus, Manny, we'd best get down there right now."

They ran as fast as men loaded down with iron could cover such a distance. Hoofed it past billiards parlors, a photo shop, McCabe's store, several cafés, and a Chinese laundry. All along the way they passed twittering women and running men headed in the opposite direction.

Three doors away from Clegg's, Longarm spotted a crumpled man lying on the store's front steps. He pushed Frazier to shelter in the doorway of a barbershop right next to the store, then forced the panting city marshal behind him. An alarmed-looking knot of people had gathered in the back of the tonsorial parlor, as far away from the front windows as possible. Longarm came to the ready and cocked both barrels of the ten-gauge.

Chapter 18

"Whaddaya see, Custis?" Frazier hissed, and brought one of his pistols up.

"Nothin'. Nothin' moving at all, Manny. Feller on the steps ain't even twitching. Looks like that fat-gutted slob that accompanied McCabe my first day in town. If he ain't deader'n a pan a used dishwater, he's damned close to it."

"How many shots did you hear?"

"Hell, I don't know. Whatever's goin' on was so far away I barcly heard anything, to tell the righteous truth. Sounded about like firecrackers. Think most a the shootin' might've occurred inside the store."

"Well, whadda we gonna do?"

"Only one choice on this list. Gotta get inside. See what the hell's waitin'. No matter what we find, though, be willin' to bet my McClellan saddle that slimy skunk Fowler McCabe's behind it."

Frazier cocked his pistol and flicked the barrel in the direction of the alley between the barbershop and Clegg's. "Tell you what, Custis, I'll go around back and sneak in the entrance for customers wantin' feed grains and such. You brace 'em from the front. Should have anybody we find in a real pinch."

Longarm snorted out a mocking chuckle. "Wouldn't be givin' me the slicker end a this nasty stick, now would you, Manny?"

"Hell, yes. You're the one with the fuckin' shoulder cannon. Big son of a bitch you're holdin' could take off the whole front of the store. Throw up a curtain a lead nobody could survive."

Longarm turned sideways. "Well, if that's the way you feel about it, you can have the shotgun, and I'll go 'round back."

Frazier held his hand up in protest. "No, thanks. Thank you very by God much. We can play it exactly the way I just described. Okay?"

Longarm grinned, then peeked around the corner and eyeballed the front door of Clegg's again. "Yeah. Works for me. You head on out. I'll wait fifteen or twenty seconds for you to get situated, then go in the front. Whatever you do, don't get feisty and shoot me by accident when we meet in the middle."

"Don't worry. You're too big and ugly to mistake for anyone else," Frazier said as he worked his way around Longarm, then carefully skirted the side of the barbershop and slipped into the litter-congested alleyway.

Longarm counted to twenty, then raised the shotgun to his shoulder and marched to Clegg's like a soldier on a drill field. He hopped onto the boardwalk, then hustled past a pile of galvanized buckets, a stack of washtubs, and a barrel of ax handles. He stepped over the corpse and, just as he'd suspected, the dead man proved to be McCabe's personal tub of lard.

From a sheltered spot beside the front door, he paused

before snatching a double-quick glance inside. Not a single item of Constance's merchandise appeared to be sitting where he'd last seen it earlier that day. And from somewhere in back of the jumbled main part of the store, perhaps near a pile of overturned boot and shoe boxes, he thought he could hear weeping.

Utilizing his best Comanche tiptoe, Longarm maneuvered across the creaking hardwood floors and gradually crept through the chaotic ruin of Frank Clegg's recent legacy. The rancid odor of spent black powder still saturated the air.

He shot a fleeting glimpse at the back wall, and spotted Manny Frazier standing in the access doorway for feed and grain sales. As Longarm watched, Pecos's city marshal holstered his pistol, then knelt at the far end of the counter on that side of the store. When he stood, he had Constance's red-nosed clerk by the elbow.

A hurried search turned up enough undamaged wooden crates for the girl to sit on. Once seated, she wiped damp eyes and a runny nose on the sleeve of her gingham dress, then readily accepted the kerchief Longarm offered.

"Her name's Emily Perkins, Custis. Her folks have a small horse and cow operation 'tween here and Barstow. I've known the family ever since they first located in the area. They've had a tough time of it. Emily took a job here to supplement her father's ranchin' efforts. For almost a year, she's been comin' in two or three days a week to work for Frank Clegg."

Longarm touched the girl on the shoulder, then squatted down in front of her so she didn't have to look up at him. He laid the shotgun on the floor, clasped his hands together, then said, "Emily, can you tell us what happened here?"

For some seconds, the girl said nothing and looked confused, as though having trouble with her memory.

Longarm took the girl's hand. "You're safe now, darlin'. Tell us what happened."

All of a sudden, the girl blurted out, "Those horrid men came back. Some of the same ones you ran off. And one man I'd never seen before. Two came in the front door, and two others entered from the back at almost the same instant." She stopped and dabbed at her running nose again.

Frazier patted the girl on the shoulder. "Then what happened, Emily? Don't be afraid now. Go on with your story. Don't leave anything out."

She nodded, but hesitated again, like a stoked engine trying to build up steam before another quick burst of energy. "Well, Miss Parker, she ran behind the counter and got her pistols. Started firing in both directions at the same time. I think she might have hit one feller just as he came through the doorway. Big-bellied man. Saw him stumble and didn't see him again after that. And she might've wounded one of those who came in from the back. Not sure. My goodness, but the noise seemed absolutely thunderous in here."

Frazier waved an arm at the room. "What caused all this damage?"

"Some of those men got to Miss Parker and snatched the pistols out of her hands. One of 'em slapped her several times. Knocked her down. Then them two others seemed to go crazy. They started yelling. Said things I didn't understand. Pushed all of Miss Parker's merchandise off the countertops. Knocked over the displays. Jerked boxes off the shelves and threw them onto the floor." She glanced around the room, a look of utter dismay on her face. "Lord Almighty, it'll take a month to pick all this stuff up."

Longarm patted the back of Emily Perkins's hand. "Was Mr. McCabe with them?"

"No. Not him, but that other man. The evil one. Barber. He was one of the two who came in from the back."

"Do you know where they went, Emily?" Frazier asked.

"No, but they took Miss Parker. Dragged her out the back into the alley, I suppose. Not sure where they went after that. Soon as they left, I just kinda fell down right here where you found me."

Longarm snatched up the shotgun and stood. "Where would they take her, Manny? You're bound to have some ideas."

"Could be anywhere, Custis. Hell, you already know that McCabe's got businesses and holdin's from Barstow to Toya. Could be anywhere."

The words had barely passed Manny Frazier's lips when Waldo Pike pushed his way through the front door. Hat in hand, he ducked his head and moved as close to the two lawmen as he could get. He slanted a quick glance back at the corpse on the store's veranda, then said, "Jus' thought you fellers would like to know, Manny. They's somethin' goin' on down at McCabe's Emporium. Not sure what, but they's an awful lot of racket inside, and folks is runnin' for cover in every direction around the place."

Longarm snatched his hat off and slapped it against his leg. "Well, that sure as hell rips the rag off the bush. That's where they took Constance. Bet McCabe didn't like it one bit either. More than likely, his men figured it'd be easy as pie to snatch Constance up and spirit her out of town. But with one dead, and another or maybe more wounded, bet those ole boys went around back and headed for the closest place they could figure to go."

For a second, Frazier looked stricken, but he quickly regained his composure. "What 'er we gonna do?"

Longarm toed at a pile of trash on the floor. "Way past time for Fowler McCabe to get the message that he can't run roughshod over folks the way he's been a-doin'."

Pecos's marshal scratched his chin and looked thoughtful. "Might be easier said than done, Custis. You may not have noticed, but there's only two of us."

Pike made a hesitant motion with one hand. "Three," he offered. "I'll stand with you, Marshal. Ain't sure what the problem is—exactly. But I'm game. Personally ain't had no use for McCabe since the time he made me fish a dollar out of an overflowin' spittoon in the Palace so's I could buy myself a drink."

Frazier dismissively waved at the only semipermanent denizen of his jail. "No need, Waldo. We can take care of it."

"Not if you're talkin' 'bout McCabe, you cain't. Not just the two of you. Gonna need all the help you can get. Looks like I might be it."

Frazier started to say something else, but Waldo stopped him. "Wasn't always a town drunk, Manny. Served as a sniper for the South in the War of Yankee Aggression, by God. And I 'uz a good 'un, too. Kilt more men than there are in this pissant town. Put a rifle in my hand and you'd be shocked at what I can do."

"You won't need a rifle. Here, take this," Longarm said, and handed Pike Constance Parker's ten-gauge, along with a double fistful of extra shells.

"Okay. Okay. 'S your show, Custis. How you wanna start this ball rollin'?" Manny said.

"We'll march right up the front of McCabe's and call 'em out. Only way to handle it now. Their little Pecos promenade has gone much too far for 'em to call back what they've done. And ain't no way they don't know the dance has gone sour on 'em."

Frazier nodded. "One good thing we've got goin' for us is that mosta McCabe's bunch is probably still out on the ranch, or in whatever other camps he's got set up for his stock-thievin' operations. Shouldn't be but three, maybe four of 'em left in town. Perhaps even fewer than that, since we've got at least one dead already."

Longarm strode to the locked gun rack built into the wall behind the counter opposite the stairway to the second floor. Unable to find a crowbar or other instrument for breaking the hasp, he pulled his pistol and blasted the lock to pieces. He yanked a pair of short-barreled coach guns from the small arsenal and handed one to Frazier. They shared the contents of a box of twelve-gauge shells. After making sure everyone was loaded and ready, they headed for the boardwalk.

Frazier and Pike trailed Longarm as the trio stepped into the street. Commerce of every sort appeared to have come to an instantaneous standstill. Horses and wagons had disappeared. The normally crowded thoroughfare was virtually deserted. Moonlike faces of anxious, inquisitive gawkers hovered in the darkened doorways and behind windows on both sides of Pecos's principal roadway.

Looking east, past Tisdale's tonsorial parlor, a tailor shop, a Chinese laundry, and a Mexican café, Longarm spotted Fowler McCabe and two of his henchmen lurking on the veranda of McCabe's massive store. All three men glanced toward Clegg's as they hastily checked the loads in their pistols.

Longarm nodded toward Frazier, then Pike, then started walking. Over his shoulder, he said, "Number matchup's looking better'n we could've dared hope, boys. Watch me. When I touch off the first shot, go for the man nearest you. I'll concentrate on McCabe."

"For a man who rarely carries a gun, McCabe's deadly, Custis," Frazier said. "Don't give 'im an inch."

Their walk ended twenty to thirty feet from the front entrance of McCabe's Store. McCabe and his heavily armed companions arrogantly stepped off the operation's raised porch and haughtily moved to within easy range of the shotguns. While McCabe's men followed their bigheaded leader without protest, Longarm noted that they appeared somewhat distressed by the action. He knew such indecision would slow them down and add to the narrow edge his group needed to succeed.

Each of the belligerent trio carried a pair of long-barreled Colt pistols strapped high on his waist. McCabe's gun rig was a fancy, hand-tooled set of double-loop Mexican holsters, decorated with silver conchos. Bone-gripped .45s jutted back and tilted at a threatening, jaunty, gunfighter's angle. Longarm turned sideways and leveled his blaster on McCabe's midsection.

Fowler McCabe's upper lip peeled away from yellowed, canine teeth. "Look at this, boys. Broke-down town marshal, well-known town drunk, and a former dead man. This the best you could do, Long?"

The hammers came back on Longarm's shotgun. "All I expect to need for the likes of you, McCabe."

"Lotta firepower you boys are carryin' there."

"You've got Constance Parker, McCabe. I want her. Have her sent out to my care, and we'll settle your hash after," Longarm sneered.

"Can't do that, Long. 'Sides, I'm tired slap to death of you, her, and the local fuckin' law as well. Hell, you hadn't even got to town 'fore you started steppin' on my corns, you badge-totin' bastard. Then the Parker woman shows up, gets a case of the hard head, and won't sell. And then you went and killed my man Tubbs. Manny and the county sheriff keep meddlin' in my business. And on and on. Feel like I've had a skunk by the tail since the day you showed your ugly face."

Manny Frazier perked up and yelled, "Throw down your weapons. Throw up your hands. You're all under arrest."

McCabe laughed out loud, then said, "For what? You cain't prove nothin', you stupid bastard."

"If Constance Parker's inside your store, and was brought there against her will, that's all I need," Longarm snarled. "Put your sorry ass in the jail, McCabe. Lucky if you don't get lynched for such abuse of a woman."

The modest amount of color McCabe's face could claim drained away like coffee poured off a saucer. "Told my man Barber to snuff her candle if this dance don't go our way, Long. Bein' as how she's already shot him, I'm pretty sure he'll be more'n happy to kill the hell outta the belligerent bitch."

Longarm gritted his teeth at the word *bitch*. "Don't be an idiot, McCabe. Might be hard for you, but give it a try. You're outgunned by a country mile. Make a wrong move and it'll be your last."

"Killin' a pissant like you's gonna be a snap, Long." With that, McCabe's hands darted for his weapons. Showing not the slightest hesitation, both his henchmen did the same. The seven-and-a-half-inch barrels of McCabe's matched cavalry-model Colts hadn't cleared leather when Longarm sent a load of heavy-duty shot into the man's chest that knocked him out of both his boots. A mistlike spray of gore flew off the man and surrounded him in a hovering wreath of instant death.

The perforated body still floated in the air like a dead leaf on the way to the ground when five more barrels of hot lead flew at his decimated gang like thousands of angry bees. McCabe's twitching corpse hit the dusty, rutted street as clouds of dust billowed up from the other gunmen's feet. A blistering curtain of lead pellets peppered their clothing, then burned through to surprised flesh. Behind them, the wooden boardwalk and storefront erupted in a shower of splinters. Some of the superheated pellets smacked into the business's front window and punched holes that left tiny rosettes of fragmented glass.

A roiling cloud of smoke, mixed with dust and sprayed blood droplets, rolled in front of Longarm and his impromptu posse like a summertime thunderstorm. He breached the coach gun, quickly reloaded, and headed through the surging screen of spent black powder for the entrance of McCabe's store.

Barely a step across the threshold, he spotted Constance Parker tied to a chair in the middle of the huge emporium. Her cheek sported a livid bruise and blood leaked from the corner of her swollen mouth. An ashen-faced Dorsey Barber stood by her side, the barrel of his pistol pressed against her temple.

Longarm could see the terror in the girl's eyes. "Put the gun down, Barber. Your friends are all shovelin' coal in Hell's furnaces. Only way out of this mess is to put that pistol aside and give me the woman."

The pasty-faced gunman clutched at a leaking wound in his side just above a single-row cartridge belt with his free hand. He swayed on unsteady feet and said, "She shot me. Ain't never been shot afore. No man's ever been lucky enough, or fast enough, to put a bullet in me. But this fuckin' woman managed it. Gonna kill her deader'n the bottom of an empty posthole."

Longarm let the shotgun slip to the floor and slowly moved his coattail away from the Colt Lightning's gleaming grips. "Never met a man yet as wanted to go to his grave marked down as a woman killer. That how you wanna be remembered, Barber?"

Bloodshot eyes in a sweat-drenched face blinked back tears of pain. "Do what I have to, lawdog. McCabe said I should kill her if'n he didn't get you. Guess I'll have to do 'er for sure now."

A pained frown flickered across the gunman's face. For the briefest of seconds, his eyes closed. His thumb came up to the hammer spur. In a flash of unparalleled speed, Longarm brought the Colt up and fired. The bullet hit his target just above the right eye. It gouged a deadly front-to-back chasm through the wounded gunman's brain, and exited in a thick gout of blood and bone that knocked his hat off and dropped his limp body to the floor like a hundred-pound sack of feed grain.

Longarm holstered his pistol, stomped over to Constance, and soon had her untied. As he helped the shaken girl to her feet, she fell onto his chest and drew him close. "I knew you would come for me. I knew you'd come," she breathed into his ear, then sagged against him. He swept her into his muscular arms and carried the limp girl onto the boardwalk.

Manny Frazier met the couple just outside the doorway. "Well, they're all goners, Long. Ain't a one of 'em got any more pulse than a busted pitchfork."

Longarm shook his head. "Tried to get McCabe to stand down. You heard me. He wouldn't have it."

Frazier smiled. "Don't worry, Marshal. Ain't a single person within fifty miles of Pecos gonna object to what happened here today."

The street was so crowded a man couldn't have swung a dead cat without hitting someone. People were as thick as yellow jackets on a spring nest. Constantly moving knots of the finger-pointing and inquisitive had poured from Pecos's shops, cafés, saloons, and stores to idly stand in the street and stare at the three shot-riddled corpses. A number of disreputable-looking types had gathered around Waldo Pike in a tight semicircle, slapping his back and nodding their approval of the gunfight's outcome.

Constance stirred in his arms as Longarm stepped into the street. Over his shoulder, he called out, "Gotta get this lady to her bed, Manny," then headed for Clegg's.

The milling crowd parted like a pasture full of cows to let him through. People stared, whispered behind their hands, and moved aside as though afraid. He strode through the throng and left them to their morbid lollygagging.

In her upstairs bedroom, he carefully laid Constance atop her bed and turned to leave. As his hand touched the cut-glass knob, she said, "Don't leave."

Propped on one elbow, the beautiful Constance motioned him back to her side. Afternoon light, filtered through a curtained window, turned her corn-colored hair into spun gold. A grateful smile spread across her bruised face. As he approached the bed again, she took his hand and pulled him down to sit beside her.

As she urged him closer, he leaned forward and covered her eager mouth with his. Their tongues dueled with one another. Her full, enthusiastic lips tasted like fresh honey and red wine. The compliant, slim-waisted, full-breasted body beneath Longarm caused an instantaneous reaction.

He sat up and said, "Are you sure about this?"

She smiled, forced a finger inside his shirt, and traced circles on his chest. "You've saved me three times in little more than a week. Such gallant behavior deserves a proper reward, good sir."

In a flurry of fiery urgency, they tore at their own clothing, and each other's, and were quickly naked. Wide-eyed, Constance stared at the rampant rod of love between Longarm's powerful thighs, flashed a toothy grin, and slid her fingers down it like an inquisitive child.

Longarm bent over, kissed and nibbled on her flawless neck, then licked his way down to the hardened tip of one heavy breast. As he sucked at the budlike nipple, her hips rose and fell in rhythmic harmony with the action of his lips. Constance's ever-inquisitive and insistent hand squeezed the thick shaft of his raging prong and guided him toward her moist, blood-engorged, waiting prize.

The triangle of incredibly long hair between her raised legs matched that on her head, except in one surprising respect. Golden to the point of being almost white, the nest of curls was velvety soft, silken, and damp with the dewy expectation of things yet to come.

He entered the waiting girl with studied care and moved in and out tenderly, until she began to writhe and struggle beneath him. Her hot breath in his ear came in rapid, clipped gasps. One arm encircled his neck and held him close; the other slid down his back until she could clasp a taut, driving buttock.

All of a sudden, Constance's entire body went stiff, then quivered uncontrollably beneath his relentless thrusting. She chewed on her already damaged lip until it bled, then, with the back of her hand, tried to smother the sounds of uncontrollable pleasure that emanated from deep within a heaving chest.

After several hours of such intense, carnal activity had passed, they lay in each other's arms, spent, covered in sweat, and ready for much-needed sleep. For the briefest of instants, Longarm let images of Denver, Billy Vail, detailed reports, mileage, meals, and other such mundane matters creep to the surface of his heaving mind. But he quickly pushed those thoughts to a back burner, then turned to Constance for another round of intense, joyous pleasure. His return to the real world could wait.

Watch for

**LONGARM IN
DEVILS RIVER**

the 361st novel in the exciting LONGARM
series from Jove

Coming in December!

And don't miss

**LONGARM AND THE
VALLEY OF SKULLS**

Longarm Giant Edition 2008

Available from Jove in October!

GIANT-SIZED ADVENTURE FROM AVENGING ANGEL LONGARM.

BY TABOR EVANS

2006 Giant Edition:
LONGARM AND THE OUTLAW EMPRESS

2007 Giant Edition:
LONGARM AND THE GOLDEN EAGLE SHOOT-OUT

2008 Giant Edition:
LONGARM AND THE VALLEY OF SKULLS

penguin.com

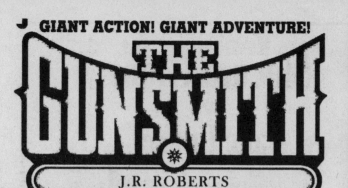

GIANT ACTION! GIANT ADVENTURE!

THE GUNSMITH

J.R. ROBERTS

Little Sureshot And
The Wild West Show
(Gunsmith Giant #9)

Dead Weight
(Gunsmith Giant #10)

Red Mountain
(Gunsmith Giant #11)

The Knights of Misery
(Gunsmith Giant #12)

The Marshal from Paris
(Gunsmith Giant #13)

penguin.com

M228AS0608

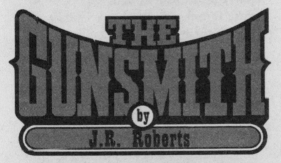